AF436693

SPIRITS

FROM THE

ELECTRONIC REALM

SPIRITS

FROM THE

ELECTRONIC

REALM

NATHAN TOULANE

Velvet Books

Velvet Books
Nathan Toulane asserts the moral rights to be identified as the author of this work.
Printed and bound in the USA

ISBN 9798824438949

© Nathan Toulane 2022
www.nathantoulane.co.uk

Author's Note

This book began my writing career—and was initially released under a different title. So, as a result, this new version has been rewritten. Re-titled. Edited, refined, and polished into this final definitive draft.

The story contains important aspects, especially the first part about people's interest in what transpires when they finally die. Henceforth, this leads to the second part of the narrative, and one man's involvement and experiments with 'Electronic Voice Phenomena', 'Spiricom', and contacting deceased individuals using the methods of tape machines, radios, videos, and electronic audio devices.

We follow Stephen Reid from early life, his meeting with colourful characters and events sending him on a discovery into the world of the paranormal and unexplained, with the drama and episodes connected with it.

The influences for this story I'll detail briefly. But, first, I would like to express profound gratitude to various authors who have written in scientific detail on the subjects of 'Electronic Voice Phenomenon' and 'Spiricom'. Although this story is fictitious, with sublime fantasy notions thrown in, I think I've been favourable to some parts of this unexplained science.

The book, *The Ghost of 29 Megacycles: A New Breakthrough in Life After Death?* I salute. It is a masterpiece of information and vital, as it helped understand methods used to contact the deceased, eloquently documented to a professional degree.

ITC is short for 'Instrumental Transcommunication'. A method of using video evidence and sound samples for proof—that there are people who've passed on to the Other Side and are now making direct visual and audible conversations with the living— and this topic figures later in the book.

My interest in this subject happened by chance when I stumbled upon Konstantin Raudive's book, *Breakthrough An Amazing Experiment In Contacting The Dead,* while in the local library. That was in 1995. Consequently, a friend and I began research and obtained results from 'E.V.P. spirit voices.' First, I concluded that the science was somewhat genuine. But then I hasten to add I wasn't sure from where these spirit voices emanated. And lastly, this stuck in my mind after receiving E.V.P. agents, menacing in tone. So, my story created a sinister character to reflect this.

After reading Konstantin Raudive's book a final time before I began this narrative, the quotations he noted from various famous and notorious figures of world history rested uneasily on the mind. The question is: *Are these genuine people who have died comforting their relatives, proclaiming they still exist in some form or another? Or are they evil entities fooling the researchers contacting them?*

QUOTE

"It may be-indeed to my mind it seems just-that, when our life has closed, when evil or good is no longer a choice for us, we may still have to witness the working out of the train of consequences we have laid. If human souls continue after death, then surely human interests continue after death. But that is merely my own guess at the meaning of the things seen."

—H.G.Wells (1866 – 1946)—

GHOSTS IN THE ATTIC

PROLOGUE

I stood in the ravaged, fire-damaged hallway, with numerous electronic devices and withered items burnt and destroyed. The mess disheartened me immensely.

A cloudy, miserable day enveloped the house, which contributed to the depression I suffered.

The boarded-up door crashed open and shut due to the mischievous wind, and the pungent smell of thick soot reeked like cremation cinders.

I stepped over a TV, burnt and cracked because of heat—in addition, an oscilloscope, plus another charred device, lay dispersed on a blackened table.

I hurried to the kitchen and observed the mess. The electric cooker rested upon its side, and other items strewn about, smashed and destroyed on the tiled ground—with two knives embedded in the wall like nails from a crucifixion.

I waited and pondered. Before, I checked somewhere different. There! I remained at the bottom of the staircase—various crushed video cameras dangled from the wall, just like nine months earlier.

Unfortunately, the set of steps had sustained too much damage. Nobody could ascend them safely.

I shook my head and released a groan of displeasure. Then ticking from a clock and putrid mist parted when I entered the lounge. Smashed ornaments greeted us. I glanced at the burnt carpet. Still wet due to water damage—caused by leaking radiators and a destroyed boiler.

Next, I headed to the dining table. Papers and documents rested atop. I fumbled through the mess and removed a damaged book. Its title: *Breakthrough An Amazing Experiment To Contact Voices From The Dead.* It flashed into my eyes because of its gold lettering.

I blew pieces of caked ash off the cover. Then avidly flicked through the literature, looking for solutions. However, most of the manuscript was unrecognisable.

Suddenly, an icy shiver crept along my back. I shocked-still. Uneasiness encircled. So, I put down the book and glanced from corner to corner. Hardly any daylight emanated from the windows, as I'd boarded them up, leaving only tiny chinks of sunlit to originate from cracked openings.

It gave the surroundings an eerie atmosphere like an Egyptian tomb.

I stood solemnly, and a dark mood rested heavily on an already shaken mind.

The terrible actions in the house had unleashed unimaginable events and caused one man to lose his life.

I questioned reason and my sanity for what I'd undertaken—as I had dabbled with something from the paranormal-occult.

At first, things seemed remarkable, but as time passed, I'd experimented with an evil force that addicted us to continue and terrified Maria, my wife, Gordon, my friend, and, inevitably, myself. I still did not even know if this ghostly entity, Mellissa, would make an unwelcome return.

When I lay on that accident and emergency table, I saw visions that could not be explained.

For the first time in life, I feared death, not the myths surrounding it, but a feeling of detachment from this earthly sphere, knowing that no loved ones could see or hear me again.

The desire of humanity to know what becomes of us when we

die and the watertight proof needed to convince sceptics, psychiatrists, and scientists that there is some kind of energy that survives when the mortal body and brain cease to function are paramount.

I thought Electronic Voice Phenomenon and Spiricom, the process of making complicated electronic machines, could have been a way to contact this realm where we are all supposed to go. That could have been the answer to many desires. Because, as a young man, I dabbled in the whole shebang. I had been a product of the sixties, the drugs, music, and fashionable clothes enjoyed without restraint.

I attained no prominent views on ghosts or ever wanted to contact phantoms; it seemed mumbo jumbo and a weirdo's paradise.

When I did army service in the 1960s, these ideas did not resonate. But they should have, as I'd witnessed fallen comrades die in agony, so maybe I ought to have been more informed, especially after the death of the old man Alfred I encountered in 'Civvy Street.'

The *Alfred* character is a significant point of this story, as he was part of my youth.

Of course, when you're young, you think the routine of the upcoming years will see you live typical society values. A stable, fulfilling life, but unforeseen occurrences can eliminate that.

My first marriage, for example, ended in divorce, mainly because of selfish moods.

But luckily, fortune smiled as another marriage to a second wife, Maria, followed.

However, after the recent turbulent adventure I'd put her through, amazingly, she had remained with us.

So therefore, readers, I think it best to begin the first part of the story, starting from the swinging sixties.

Chapter One

I waited nervously near the British army's office room. I then glimpsed at my watch before peering through the door slit.

A clerk sat at a shabby wooden desk, signing discharge papers. "Private Reid!' he shouted. 'In here Now!' I nodded, then marched.

The army clerk glanced with indifference. He passed the discharge documents. 'Mind signing here!'

Angry shouting erupted from the Parade-Ground as the Sergeant-Major berated new recruits. This distracted my attention before the clerk cleared his throat. 'What you waiting for, boy! Applause! Complete the task.'

'Oh! Sorry! Yes, sir,' I replied. I signed the papers and, with expectation, prepared to exit.

The guy in authority had the last laugh. 'Good luck in civvy street, Reid. You're gonna need it!'

'Thank you,' I replied, not appreciating the remark. Outside, I exhaled with relief and continued along the corridor to freedom.

I drifted from the present moment and pondered. *'God knows what I'm going to do? Anyway, I can't complain! Seeing I've had a free holiday round many countries. With the help of her majesty's pound and the Sergeant-Major's boot implanted up my arse!'*

I purchased a second-class ticket to Kings Cross London at the railway station in town and headed towards Platform Seven. The atmosphere at the station was eerily quiet. I paced impatiently, causing my freshly shined army boots to grind and scratch on the concrete floor.

Due to fatigue, I sat on a bench which graced the platform. Then removed a freshly rolled cigarette before striking a match on the floor. A flame arose. Then I inhaled deeply and whispered inner questions. 'Stepfather's gonna love our meeting. He wanted us army bound. But why? Done four years of infantry service. In the big wide world now. And I want adventure. The sixties' revolution and liberation are next on the cards. Wanna experience its delights. Trendy clothes. And the music and events happening in this fantastic period of freedom.'

I coughed croakily when smoke from the cigarette travelled the wrong way.

Minutes passed, and then the sound of a train approached, juddering into the station. I ascended, lifted my cases, and entered the carriage.

The train jerked, and a journey began, taking me inevitably towards Civvy Street.

Further, into the trip, we passed through Leicester, Loughborough and other vibrant towns and cities.

Wiping the condensation from the dirty carriage window, I peered through the hazy blur with a thoughtful expression, unaware of what would happen when I arrived at the stepfather's house. My eyes waned heavily as tired—I drifted into a pained sleep.

'Pound! That do?' I remarked.

'Yeah, son! Be perfect,' replied the cabbie in his cockney accent. Money was exchanged, and off sped the taxi.

I remained at the gate, then hastened to the stepfather's house. The cunning swine had been watching because he yanked ajar the door.

His face went agitated. Manner abrasive. 'Ah. Back then! Came crawling like a waster. Couldn't take it. Eh?'

I angrily barged aside. The stepfather stumbled backwards, knocking into the ornate cabinet.

'That's nice!' I said. 'Your diplomacy stinks! Make a good tyrant!' I edged into the hallway. Bang! The heavy door crashed shut. I spun around. Shocked. Dismayed.

'Come here. Varmint!' he screamed.

'*Christ sake!* Knock it off! Been riding the damn train for hours.'

'If you think you're staying here. Forget it! Matey,' he said, breath reeking like a sewer. 'You joined the army for queen and country. To uphold empire. Fight the communists. Battle the Russians! Had a good chance to build a career. Yet! Chucked it away.'

My left fist curled into a fist. 'Listen! Pal! Done everything for her majesty. I've had it! Through. Y'know! Sick of this. Just returned. And you've started. On and on. Like a rabbit shagger. Save perverted crap,' I added, 'on how to live a life. Because yours! Lives in a bottle of rum!'

'Don't answer back!' he yelled. 'I won't stand for bare nosed cheek! You're not gonna wind up as an idle bastard. Rocking to shit music. Composed by piss heads. Parading on motorbikes and scooters. Then brawling on Brighton beach with your buddies.'

I slammed the heavy suitcase into his boot.

'*ARGH!* You've broken me *bleedin* foot!'

Then mother's voice exploded. 'Stuff and nonsense, George! What on earth!?'

I laughed. Hysterically. 'Sorry. Mate!'

Abruptly, he about-faced. Cursed. Then, loud and curt, bawled, 'Right. That settles it… out yer go tomorrow. Bag and baggage! Yer get me!'

Mother descended the stairs, spoke a comment, and ushered George to the kitchen.

Now my stepfather had never been a diplomat. Suppose ever since I caught him years back, giving the vicar's wife, Esmeralda, a good seeing to. It's amazing. Even when I saw him, he denied it. Declaring, he was practising a new first-aid technique.

He ruled mother with lies and deceit ever since she married him on the rebound after the death of my real father, who served with gallantry in Africa.

I wish he were still alive. My father would never have treated us in this pig shot way.

Later on, I wandered round town when the sound and smells from a pub, *The King George,* drew us to its doors.

It appeared quiet. An elderly man sat in the corner and briefly caught my *eye*. Instantly, I marched to the counter and asked the Bartender for a drink. 'What's the poison?' queried the Barman.

'Beer! Your best!' I exhaled a sigh, and itchy fingers tapped the counter.

He slammed down the glass. 'There! Enjoy.' I gave the money and sipped. It tasted terrific, and I certainly needed a pick-me-up after recent events.

I drank a couple of pints throughout the early evening and gazed aimlessly around the bar for female companionship.

'Hey, son! Got a light?'

Startled, I noticed the *same* elderly gentleman I caught sight of earlier. Thus, I was destined to meet Alfred. I headed to the table, struck a match for his pipe, and remained silent.

'Not got much to say,' said the old man. 'What's doing! Seems the entire world rests on those shoulders.'

'Why should you care?' I replied, voice soft, as I sat opposite. 'No one's spoken to us all night. Ain't even a decent woman in here to banter with.'

'Well. I'm talking to ya!'

'So, what! You're just an old geyser. Gonna lecture on the good old days. You lot live in the past. Bang on about loyalty. The glorious dead. And war and empire.'

'Rubbish! Trying to make conversation.' Alfred pointed his tobacco-stained finger. 'Now! I'll tell anyone to their face. What I think. I speak the truth. Nail the fakes.' His voice arose. 'Maybe, that's why I don't want friends.'

The Barman stared with mocking disdain.

The old man continued. 'Drunk or sober. You'll know exactly how I feel.'

I gazed with amusement, thinking, *Why am I sitting here talking to this stupid guy?* I prepared to exit as I found his conversation irritating. Suddenly, he grabbed us. 'You're in trouble!' His tone changed. 'See it in the eyes! What's wrong?'

'Well. Not normally discourteous. Just pissed off. Done army service. Seen the colonies. Visited places I only dreamed of. So now that I'm a civilian, thought life could only get better.'

'So! Problem is?'

'Stepfather! Wanted us army bound. Do added service. When the four-year *contract* ended. But I was through! Had enough.' I took stock. 'Wish now I'd remained. If this is what civilian life represents.' My tone enraged. 'Mean bastard threw a tirade of insults. Only got back this morning. Had a massive row. Now he's thrown us on the streets!'

'Mmm. Ha!' Alfred chuckled.

'What's funny?'

Alfred scratched his baldhead. 'You are!'

'Why. What's the gag?'

Alfred philosophically moaned. 'So much of life left to live. Look what awaits me?' There followed a thoughtful pause before he spoke solemnly, '… The Grave…'

Alfred removed some old coins. 'Grab two pints. By the way. What name do you go by?'

'Stephen Reid,' I replied, 'Incidentally. What's yours?'

'Alfred!' He opened his greasy palm, and we shook hands.

I pointed at the Barman behind the counter, indicating I wanted two pints. The Barman went flushed and coarse. 'Hang on! Only got one pair of hands! Busy doing drinks.'

'Here!' I uttered impatiently. 'Move it. I'm parched!'

The Barman shrugged—various things were on his mind. 'What'll be, Miss?' he asked a young lady. He then continued being a creep to her. 'And perhaps. Maybe later. Fancy hitting the town? I'd be honoured to have such attractive beauties on either arm?'

I huffed, and my attention drifted before I noticed several people enter. Various sounds of laughter, merriment, and talking ascended. I glanced at the Barman. He seemed to have trouble with the women, one of whom had a grating, posh voice. 'A gin and tonic!' she barked. 'And one vodka! With a slim line tonic.' Her eyes went wild. 'I specifically stated that!'

However, the Barman had cocked up the drinks. He placed the beverages in front of the ladies, and the outcome went frenzied.

The woman gave a vile stare. Winced. Then exclaimed, 'Here! Not drinking that! Normal tonic in it… I wanted a slim line.'

The Barman and this woman argued, and uproar arose within the pub.

'Give us a break! Spare a copper for a hard man.'

'Slim line tonic! Nothing else!'

'Come on. Please! No! It's not on. Don't need this shit! Bollocks, you tarts!' This quarrel went on for a few minutes before the women exited the scene.

In the meantime, the Barman prepared fresh drinks. 'Now! Where they gone?' he growled.

'Can't you guess? Left.' I pointed at the women.

'Hey!' he screamed, but it was too late. They'd scarpered. The Barman erupted. 'Flaming arseholes! Stinking slags!' His posture, enraged, skin flushing red. 'Bloody lousy slags! Hate this job—idiots wasting time… Idiots! Everything's bollocks.'

He continued cursing repeatedly, shook his head in disgust, and his eyes met mine with a scowl. 'Two pints. Wasn't it?'

'Yeah,' I replied timidly, trying not to rile him. 'Hope you ain't inconvenienced?' The Barman wheezed and grumbled as he did the drinks. Next, he slammed them flat—lent across the bar, and huffed as I gave payment.

Quietly and slyly, he spoke. 'Noticed. Y'know? You sat in the corner. Talking to that git. Alfred! Take advice. Steer well clear.' He gave an arrogant glance.

'Why?' I asked, puzzled.

'Because he's *er* crazy old sod. Mind's pickled with alcohol. Tells make-believe stories. Unbelievable to a rational man. What with him. And his fat old cousin. The arrogant cow.'

'Not married then?' I asked with doubt.

The Barman began emptying ashtrays. 'Course not!' he replied. 'Who'd you think would tolerate him?'

'You're a slight judgmental.'

'Oh, piss off!' Then he stepped aside to serve another customer.

As I sat opposite Alfred, he quipped, 'Trouble with Trevor the Barman?'

'Nothing I can't handle. Seems impatient. Lacks the human spirit.'

Alfred sipped his pint. 'Heed this son,' he stated. 'I languished in the military. Did but eight years.'

'That's incredible?' I said suspiciously. Alfred relayed a story; I did not know if it was true but withheld opinion.

As a young man, aged eighteen, his father and mother sent him to his grandmothers, but instead, he visited a local Recruiting Centre. Signed papers. And joined the infantry.

He was fast-tracked into service and Posted to South America to fight rebels in the jungle.

Hilarious, I thought. As Alfred never mentioned what he did in the weeks beforehand. So, I thought it best to keep my council.

After rings of pipe smoke, he continued with his yarn about the army. Apparently, he returned years later with a wife in tow.

A couple of minutes transpired, and I observed his face, examining the defects. The only hair that remained on his scalp— was bushy tufts around the ears. He muttered that the top of his head blistered red in the summer due to sunburn and attracted annoying flies and other insects. Next, I noticed a big white bandana hanging from his pocket. 'Is that what that accessory is for?'

'You betcha! Keeps the sun off me bonce.'

Because of monotony, I re-studied Alfred's features, which triggered amusement. It had a rather beaten, English bulldog expression. You could say it resembled someone who'd been chewing a wasp.

I lit a cigarette and noted Alfred's nose, which had an indentation. 'How an earth! I mean…. Your conk? Nose is deformed?'

Alfred went angry. 'Now then! Gonna rant on about looks? You ain't a pretty picture.'

I drew a hand across my cropped hair. 'Sorry! But at least I've still got a mop. Covers the scalp. No bald patches yet.'

Alfred regained composure and explained his nose broke when he got into a fight with a mate. And his cousin, Victoria, reset it wrongly.

'Where does Victoria live?'

'In our house,' replied Alfred. He stated it wasn't much but suited them perfectly. She took care of his requests and kept the place spick and span.

Alfred's eyes blurred, and I suspected boredom surfacing. He yawned. However, it was then—I observed his remaining teeth; he only had a few protruding from the lower jaw.

'Not many canines, doing?'

Alfred closed his mouth. 'I know. Their sole purpose. Is to support this pipe.' He majestically placed the object in his mouth, acting as the *King of England* and sucked. To me, he looked like a baby chewing a dummy.

After a lingering pause, Alfred posed a question. 'Now, Stephen! You've nowhere to go. Thrown out, by your stepfather. Well! A spare room's going. Come. Stay with Victoria and I. You're quite—' Suddenly, the pub's main doors banged apart, interrupting Alfred, and in trod a heavy rough-looking guy who resembled a criminal docker. To be frank, he's someone you wouldn't want to bump into on a dark night.

Then, he ripped the power chord from the flashing jukebox to add insult to injury.

The Docker shouted. Raged! His words packed with menace. 'Who's the piece of shit? Called me wife a slag?' A pause transpired before the slam of a fist on a table ignited the atmosphere. 'Out with it! Waiting for the culprit to show his ugly mug! She wanted drinks. But got abused. By a scumbag—scallywag!'

The entire bar went silent. Murmurings from customers turned into accusations—and I guessed the Barman had identified the poor soul.

Alfred and I glanced at Trevor the Barman. Then abruptly, a few sinister men entered.

Ominously, they searched the pub. Seeking vengeance. Before halting beside their thuggish leader.

At that moment, the reflection from a mirror caught the Docker's gaze. And suddenly, he identified the culprit: Trevor.

The Docker hurried to the counter. 'Bastard! Bastard!' he yelled. 'Gave the missus a lousy drink! Labelled her a slag! Didn't ya!'

'Correct, Mate,' replied the Barman. 'Deserved it. For wasting time! I'm nobody's doormat!'

'Not your mate. Understand!!!' replied the Docker. He drew breath, eyes wild with rage.

Instantly, drinks on the counter tipped over, spilling beer everywhere.

'Oh, no! Prepare for the showdown!' muttered Alfred. On that last word, mayhem exploded. Glasses cracked against the walls, and thuds rang out like masters thumping servants.

Immediately, the Docker dragged the Barman across the counter, grabbed his throat, and threw a punch. It cricked the Barman's jaw.

In the kerfuffle, tables flew, and a man tried to intervene. However, a hard kick in the groin sent the unfortunate soul onto the table where I sat.

Alfred winced and spat out his pipe; while hysterical women panicked and screamed.

The Barman threw punches, but the Docker beat them aside.

After that, the Docker held the Barman tight. First, in a headlock and he unleashed a flurry of blows. Next, both staggered, cries rang out, and bar stools fell into puddles of sloshing beer.

Then, the shady characters that accompanied the Docker got stuck in. Glasses, bottles and ashtrays travelled throughout the air, accompanied by clouts, dull thuds, and breaking glass.

Finally, the bar resembled a seventeenth-century gin house, complete with lawlessness.

Alfred dug his tobacco-stained fist into my arm. 'Quick. Let's escape.'

I nodded. We upped and hurried to the pub's exit. However, the struggling Barman and Docker knocked into us. This incensed me, so I barged against them.

Both staggered backwards and collapsed upon an upturned table, straight into the laps of some unfortunate locals. Then women's voices in the pub screamed, 'For Gawd's sake! Call the police! These lunatics are wrecking the place.'

Alfred and I exited and took stock. Nevertheless, the lawlessness within the drinking den continued. Ale and wine glasses, plus other objects, soared and split apart—shattering into pieces. 'I presumed,' I said breathlessly. 'This was a quiet Inn. Y'know. Respectable?'

Alfred brushed himself down. 'Course it ain't. Only go in there for the cheap beer! Believe you, me. No quiet life exists in that pub.'

'Yes, but I thought—' I was stopped in full sentence by the shattering of glass and the strange sight of the Barman hurtling through the main window. He hit the ground with a dull thud and landed dazed and bloodstained on the pavement, with the cynical Alfred and me observing.

The Barman groaned and moaned, 'Oh… ah. Owl. Oh!'

Alfred walked, eyed him with disdain, chuckled, and while making a sucking noise from the lungs, spat black stained mucus onto the Barman's forehead. The Barman's eyes flickered open, and he gnashed his crooked teeth, 'Why you bastard!' he screamed. 'Filthy scumbag! I'll KILL YOU! You hear me! I'll tear that head off. And shit down your…'

I tugged Alfred's jacket and thought it best to run before he killed us. So we both rushed along the road while a police bell sounded in the distance.

'Move it!' I protested. 'Police approaching.'

The old man chuckled.

'Why gob on his head?' I said, astonished. 'You knew he was pissed?'

'Deserved it!' replied Alfred. 'Never liked us. Ever since I told him, what an arrogant swine he be!'

After a heated exchange, he asked, 'did I want to rent the spare room in his house?' With alcohol and the previous events of the evening clouding my judgment and nowhere else to go tomorrow, I accepted the offer: Alfred's address was *24 Runcorn Road.*

So, after saying goodbye, Alfred hurried to his residence. Consequently, I prepared to return to the stepfather's house, pack my stuff, and depart the following day.

Chapter Two

It was two o'clock in the afternoon. I hastened along the uneven pavement while carrying a big brown suitcase.

I checked the writing on the piece of paper. So, this must be the address, I figured. I strolled on. Stopped, then looked at the house with the number *29* written in thick chalk.

The dirty nets in the windows caught attention; the front door dull and grotty. And an old, fat woman's face appeared in one window before disappearing.

With anxiety, I knew this must be Alfred's home. It did not impress, but with nowhere else to live, I let out a hefty sigh, progressed the path through weeds and overgrown grass, and stood at the entrance.

No reply arose when I knocked on the door. I waited, then hit again. I was about to return to the bus stop, guessing I'd arrived at the wrong address when I heard shouts.

'Are you going to get the door? Silly old cow? You're sending me barmy!'

I cringed with embarrassment, for I knew it was Alfred's rabid tones.

The front door creaked ajar, and Victoria's powdered, wrinkled features appeared. 'You must be Stephen,' she uttered in a cackling voice. 'Enter! Me and Alfred are glad you came.'

I nodded. Advanced and went to the lounge. I noticed Alfred resting in a green armchair, puffing on his pipe. Then, abruptly, he rose, 'Stephen! Stephen. Good to see ya. Grab a seat.'

I placed the bulky case on the floor and slumped into a chair. Finally, I felt satisfied that the burden of bus rides and other excursions was over.

Victoria waddled in. 'Nice cup of tea. Young man?'

'That'd be great. Thanks.'

Victoria shuffled into the kitchen, humming and singing. Looking upon the room and thinking with various notations, I observed the old lady—making detailed assessments.

My first *opinion* of Victoria came as a surprise. A plump lady. Very much the opposite of Alfred on the physical scale, him slender in torso, and I reckon a few years her junior. Her obesity, though, did not hinder her agility.

Alfred released a smoker's cough, his lungs fighting countless chemicals. 'Say,' he wheezed. 'What's on that mind, Stevy? Don't mind the nickname?'

'No. Not at all,' I joked.

'You'll like it here,' he remarked. 'Victoria's done the spare room. And everything is fine.'

'Thanks! So, grateful I've escaped the stepfather. Hopefully, for good. Perhaps I'll get peace now.'

Alfred bent to a trivial side table and removed a notepad and pen. 'Right! For the rent.'

After I paid Alfred money, his cousin, Victoria, entered with a pot of tea and a tray of freshly baked cakes.

****

In the evening, we had dinner and talked—with Alfred and Victoria in splendid form. But I was tired and readied an excuse to retire to the spare room.

I got into bed and left the inadequate gas mantle on, for I always feared the dark. Mind you, the damn lighting the mantle released was unnerving.

While tossing and turning and trying to sleep, I heard footsteps approach. 'Who's there?'

The bedroom door creaked ajar. 'Alfred! That you?'

'No! Victoria,' she uttered in her distinct cackling voice. 'Brought a grand cup of drinking chocolate.'

I thanked her, and she exited, closing the creaky door. I picked up the drink and drank. 'Oh, *Christ*!' I fumed. My taste buds contracted. And face contorted in agony. This awful concoction contained salt instead of sugar. I retched and *thought* Victoria was senile.

Anyway, things cannot get worse, I thought. So, I tried settling for a good night's sleep.

Everything seemed quiet at three o'clock in the morning when abruptly wailing singing ascended. It resembled a mad opera singer with piles.

Grumbling and thinking, *Who could be responsible for this awful noise?* I squinted and opened my eyes. However, the singing continued.

I glanced at the clock by the side of the bed: three-fifteen in the morning displayed. Yet, this constant wailing continued for the next two hours.

I tried to sleep, but could not, no matter how hard I tried. By what means anybody could rest with this noise beggared belief.

Lastly, I cursed and heard Alfred yell. 'Stick a sock in it! You stupid old fat cow!'

Then a barrage of foul language trailed with powerful effect.

Suddenly banging sounds on the walls, and the muffled shouts from a raging man, interrupted. 'HEY! CUT IT OUT! PEOPLE TRYING TO SLEEP!' It came from one of the unlucky next-door neighbours. Nevertheless, Alfred continued screaming and shouting.

'Victoria! You're sending everyone round the twist. Stupid bag. You're—'

The male neighbour went completely mad and roared, 'I'll Commit Murder! I Will Commit Murder.'

Then, high in pitch, a woman's cry erupted, 'No… Jack! Don't. He's nuts. No!'

I shoved my head under a pillow. However, Alfred took it upon himself to whistle, which carried on for ages. Then, suddenly, the neighbour's patience snapped. 'I CAN'T STANDDD!!! *THIS!*

The massive smash of an object shattered against the wall of Alfred's house; it must have been of tremendous weight, for it shook the entire foundations. My thoughts went into overdrive.

'What've I done? Living with a bunch of raving nutters.' I groaned, then continued. 'In heaven's name. I swear, I'm cursed?'

I felt sleep weary and had momentary sickness. Then I closed my eyes for relief. Desperate for forty-winks—and prayed for the noise to cease.

At breakfast, I said very little. Opposite sat Victoria and Alfred, eating their brunch with frequent slurping noises and the odd feature of breaking wind in stereo.

I noticed Victoria's false teeth fighting to digest food; they seemed to possess a mind of their own.

Alfred dipped a piece of bread into his porridge and uttered, 'Pleasant night?'

'You're joking! What was that commotion? Early morning?'

Alfred seemed apologetic. 'Sorry. Our Victoria loves bursting into song in the early hours. So afraid, you're gonna have to lump it.' He then smiled at his cousin. 'Told ya he'd love it here.'

Victoria poured tea and mumbled, 'Yeah! I know.' Bewilderment enveloped us because of their strange mannerisms.

Alfred glanced thoughtfully. 'There's everything in porridge that a man needs. And before you read Karl Marx. Read The Four Values Of Capitalism.'

I felt confused—but countered, 'Whatever. You are the boss.'

Unfortunately, Victoria released her awful screeching laugh with a quick burst of breaking wind, which I found ghastly.

I wondered if any unfortunate boyfriend had experienced the pleasure of her breaking wind on their leg while they were a bed.

Then Victoria asked, 'whether I had anything planned?' I said, 'I would try asking in town to see what jobs were going.' I knew I needed money to sustain myself. Seeing the army pay was exhausted.

Alfred spoke with optimism as I rose from the breakfast table, its blue patterned cloth decorated with tea stains.

'You'll find something. There's always things going round district… Many a more, or many a day as the local priest used to say to his big dog as it squatted for a shit.' I laughed in stunned amusement at his comments, exited the scene, and prepared to find a job.

Chapter Three

About eight months passed. I had gained employment as a warehouse driver. But gradually, the toil of living with Alfred and Victoria affected the nerves. I never felt comfortable bringing a lady back, as I could never get the old characters to venture to a pub or other social setting in the evening.

I needed space as I wanted a home of my own. I had to escape to a place of solitude and have privacy returned.

I would not tell Alfred and Victoria of these intentions until I'd signed a tenancy agreement, and possibly one night, I'd disappear from their company.

At dusk, I sat in the murky living room beside the grubby fireplace, with the towering flames burning and giving feelings of warmth.

Victoria rested upright on the green chair opposite, and Alfred fiddled about the room. 'Work treating you well? Seven months now!' he said while adjusting the worn gas mantle.

'Yep! Fine,' I replied while observing the dim light. I glanced to the four corners of the lounge. It was dire. I'd *told* Alfred, on numerous occasions, he must get electricity installed for the house before he burnt the place down. Gas made the area unsafe, and the lighting—well, if you could call it light, what with cinders from the fire, coal puffs, plus Victoria and Alfred's smoking—overall, it resembled a pollution ridden smog.

Alfred spoke with the usual ignorance, '*Naa!* Does us fine? That's the way it is. And that's the way I want it.' He lit his big pipe and continued, 'Anyway, Stevy. Gotta ask something. By chance. You learn a trade. In the army?'

'Not really,' I remarked with an edge of deference. 'The infantry was my game. All you learned. Was to kill! Kill in a gruesome number of ways. Plus, endless cleaning. And removing rubbish. Before getting a punch in the mouth from the sergeant or corporal if he was having a bad day. They'd do this if they'd not gotten their leg over with the local tarts from town.'

Alfred turned to Victoria and told her to grab a couple of ale cans from the fridge.

Next, Alfred blew puffs of smoke from his pipe and said 'that he'd been an engineer while in the army. Servicing tanks and military trucks.'

I did not believe it and teased him sarcastically, 'Come off it! You ain't a mechanic. Takes special skills to be competent—in that field.'

Alfred pointed to a 'military certificate' hanging on the lounge wall. I arose and examined it, thinking it was a fake, but it was genuine.

As I took a seat, Alfred said he had performed a repair job on Winston Churchill's car. All with the aid of a screwdriver. Ground to a knife-edge. A spanner. And special motor oil. This procedure kick-started Churchill's car, and the Wartime Leader continued his journey to the Houses of Parliament. It must have been true as Alfred passed a picture with Churchill giving the famous thumbs up. 'Good lord. Never knew,' I said. 'You're a man of surprises.'

'Nice to know. Achieved something worthwhile. Other than drinking exploits. Seeing I reside in the winter of years.' He removed a handkerchief and blew his nose.

Victoria was tired. She bid 'goodnight' and retired upstairs. Then a mellow silence transpired. Alfred seemed to be in a reflective mood. He poked us in the arm. 'Stephen. It's perfect she's hit the sack. Something I wanna discuss. Most important.'

'What's the trouble?' I replied.

Homely comforts briefly interrupted us. The first fall of winter rain announced its arrival by hitting the window overlooking the garden, and the antique clock chimed, accompanied by sizzling wood burning on the fire.

'Seriously,' asked Alfred emotionally. 'What'd you think becomes of us… Beyond the grave?'

'That's an odd question!' I chuckled. 'There's nothing! When you're dead! Finished! No angels. No harps. No living in the clouds with religious saints.'

Alfred protested. 'Stevy, boy—I gotta know. Is there something? Anything. After death?'

I assumed Alfred was a sceptic. I never thought religion inspired him or he had any supernatural notions. Personally, I believed it was bullshit! As I often argued with the army chaplain, who used to say categorically, 'It is fine to kill' and other ridiculous philosophies. This only intensified my dismissive viewpoint on the subject.

'I believe in ghosts,' said Alfred sternly. 'Cause I witnessed one.'

'Don't be ridiculous. No such thing.'

'It's true! Seriously. Believe us.'

'Alright. So, a ghost scared ya! What exactly you getting at?'

The old man went solemn. 'Now, son. Whoever of us dies first. And breaks free from this mortal coil, will somehow find a way to let the other know, they've survived! And make a *sign* showing a spirit world exists. Beyond this life of grief and tears.'

I must admit I had no idea about Alfred's pessimism on existence. So, I was flippant. 'Don't talk daft! Even the psychic debunker *Houdini* promised to let friends know he'd survived death. Especially to his wife, *Bess*. But there's no evidence he ever achieved this. From what I've read.'

'That may be the case,' Alfred questioned glumly. 'But I mean what I state.' A thoughtful pause occurred—then a *phrase* came like a biblical quote. "Time is the essence. For the rest of my Duties". These will be the words I'll use to proclaim that I have survived death.'

Alfred had a tear in his eye. '*Time is the essence. For the rest of my duties,* remember Stevy?'

I felt sceptical, but in the end, agreed. Alfred also asked If I would sort out financial matters and care for Victoria when he died. He glanced with a wistful expression at her picture next to himself on the ornate mantelpiece.

I was hesitant but promised to carry out these wishes.

The coal fire, mixed with wood burning in the dirty fireplace, faded, and I glimpsed at the clock—the evening had flown by.

I arose—to exit the scene and get rest. But before I went to bed, I told Alfred that I'd be away for a couple of weeks; and staying with an old chum, Mick, from my army days.

'Two weeks!!!' berated Alfred.

'I know,' I replied as I stepped near the door. 'Be going early morning. Hopefully. I'll miss the delights of Victoria's opera crescendo.'

While telling me not to work too hard, Alfred guffawed. 'Have a good time, mate. Wish you luck. Also! Gonna try an get your leg over with some fat woman or trollop?'

'I beg your pardon!!!'

Alfred unleashed a wild laugh.

I didn't get his sense of humour, especially after talking about *death* for most of the evening. However, I quipped, 'Don't worry, Alfred. I'll try.' Then I bid goodnight.

Four o'clock the following morning, I quietly shut the door and hurried along the path. I turned behind and heard Victoria bursting into song.

Alfred started screaming and shouting, and the neighbours' lights flicked on in a domino fashion.

I chuckled and thought with amusement. *They are a right pair; got eccentric, compulsive personalities. Mind you.* I paused as their screaming and shouting broke the pleasant sound of morning birdsong. *I can't accuse them of senile dementia. Both are too colourful and, on the ball, for material needs for surviving and paying their way. I wish I'd not made that 'stupid promise' to Alfred, agreeing that I'd take care of Victoria if any mishap or illness befell him. But I suppose after a few weeks, he will have forgotten about it with a bit of luck. As he trudges round the various ale houses, he often frequents.*

Chapter Four

T*he Flag and Dog* pub began emptying its usual colourful characters. Eleven o'clock in the evening meant 'Last Orders.'

Alfred was his typical drunken self as he set upon his routine journey home. Loud singing emerged in the background, and a fellow customer told Alfred to be careful as he'd had a skinful that evening.

Further on, along a dimly lit street, staggering and smiling, he jabbered, 'Crikey, what a night! What a wonderful night.'

He passed a narrow shady alley with not much consideration, but waiting there was Trevor the Barman, the guy Alfred spat on weeks ago.

Trevor stepped from the lane, his metal toecap shoes grinding on the pavement.

Suddenly a dog's ugly howl serenaded with drunken cries and sinister echoes wailed while dustbins tumbled to their doom in the distance. An eerie wind followed, whistling like mad ghosts before Trevor scratched his unshaven chin, eyeing Alfred menacingly, and grinned like the devil himself.

'Now! I'll give him what for,' he growled. 'Something to remember us by.' He trailed Alfred menacingly, steps crushing gravel underfoot.

The older man thought he heard breathing. He stopped. Turned.

'Anyone there? Arthur. That you?' He *stared* into the darkness but saw nothing. So, continued.

The Barman paced quicker, gnashing yellow teeth while rubbing his sweaty clenched fist with a metal knuckle-duster.

Alfred heard angry footsteps approaching. The old man knew he had to make a break for it. 'Leave me alone!' he exclaimed fearfully. 'Get away!' Alfred detoured behind a demolition area and stumbled over slabs of rubble. He twisted his neck. A click! He stared. Eyes widening. Chest tightening, and his legs turned to jelly.

Alfred's gaze unfocused when a dark human shape sidestepped within the shadows.

Instantly the Barman sneaked ahead and positioned parallel.

The old man's head pointed. Then suddenly, and with a facade of horror—he faced Trevor.

Immediately, the old man's shirt ripped apart, and Trevor growled, 'Bided me time. Been looking forward to this moment.' He flung his forearm across Alfred's shoulder and caught him with a devastating punch. The fatal blow smashed Alfred's eye socket. The old man screamed, the force of the strike— overwhelming.

Alfred threw both hands aloft and clung tight. Desperation kicked in. He gripped Trevor's hair; both struggled. Then a multitude of kicks smacked his shins. 'Take the wallet. Please! *PLEASEEEE!*' Abruptly the old man's trousers split during the struggle, and his pocket watch fell to the ground.

Trevor had fire in the belly. Warped revenge in the soul. He seemed to enjoy this humiliating, degrading behaviour. He snarled. 'Feel better. Do you! Revenge is a dish best served by a fist. Proved that tonight.' He laughed and punched Alfred firmly in the stomach, which sent the elderly victim sideways.

Alfred staggered, then tripped on bricks, hitting the rocky, dusty ground with a thump.

A couple of people's voices in the distance circled, and Trevor thought someone had spotted him, so he beat a hasty retreat from the scene. 'Enjoyed that! Hope that sticks the old geyser in the grave. Settles him in the earth!' Then he made his escape into the shadows and moonlit night.

Alfred groaned and doubled in agony. He released coughs and heavy breaths, anything to soothe the distress. 'My legs. Stomach! So much pain. *SO MUCH PAIN!*' He touched his jaw and vomited beer-drenched bile.

Luckily, a man and woman were 'chatting nearby.' He shouted for 'assistance.' The couple heard the cry and dashed to his aid. The man's gaze lowered. 'Mate!' he asked, shocked. 'You alright?'

The man beckoned at his girlfriend. '*Christ,* Shelia! Guy's taken a hammering.'

Alfred, beset with agony, spoke. 'Please! Someone mugged us. Try to get me home.' He fought the pain in his chest and took a breath.

First, the man and woman lifted Alfred. Next, he gave them directions. Then finally, the three of them struggled to his house. Eventually, they arrived at the entrance.

Victoria *heard* a loud knock; she made her way from bed and went downstairs. She adjusted the hall gas mantle and opened the door. There! She witnessed Alfred supported by the couple. He was panting, blood dripping from his mouth.

Immediately, she screamed. '*ALFREDDDDDDDD!!!*'

I'd been absent for two weeks, and what a hectic time. Nevertheless, after many queries—I'd found a flat. Thus, I would tell Alfred and Victoria that I would be leaving.

I knocked on their old front door and waited. *Strange,* I thought. *Usually, hear Alfred shouting and hollering* at *Victoria.* I knocked again. The door creaked ajar, and Victoria appeared, detached from reality. Well, that was my conclusion.

'Stephen,' she said, relieved. 'Oh! Dear… please. Enter.'

'How're things?'

Victoria was pale and drawn.

'What's the problem?' I continued as I hurried to the lounge.

Victoria closed the door, followed, and rested on a chair, exhaling wearily.

'Where's old grumpy?' I said flippantly. 'Don't say. Let me guess. Down the pub! Boozing!'

Victoria shook her head and said Alfred lay upstairs. Put to bed. I asked, 'What's he doing there?'

She removed a tissue and blew her nose. 'Alfred's had an accident. Night after you left. Fell on uneven pavement. But I reckon he took a beating. Go upstairs and have *er butchers*. Because I've had terrible trouble. The doctor's been, but Alfred reckons he knows everything and told him to get lost! I worry so much,' added Victoria. 'It's such heartbreak. He's selfish! Stubborn! I don't know what to do.'

I told her I'd check him out.

'Y'know,' said Victoria. 'He's made me go back and forth to the shops. Wanted countless things. Stated drinking neat vodka is good for the chest. Warm rum cures insomnia. And whiskey helps ease stomach pain. But, it's tiring,' she added. 'I worry for me hip. Doing these ridiculous errands.' She released a heavy breath and rubbed her ankle. We talked further before I exited upstairs.

I approached Alfred's bedroom and waited, then gradually opened the door. The strawberry-coloured curtains were half-drawn, and cups, bottles and pills were scattered everywhere. 'You awake?' I whispered.

The old man grunted and strained.

I helped as best I could—trying to avoid the objects on the floor.

Alfred coughed. 'Been in the wars. Boy! Suppose you can say. You'd not believe how swollen I am. How tender the stomach is. Aches like a festering wound.'

I approached, and after careful examination, he looked dreadful. His right eye swollen like a snooker ball, while the rest of his features painted black and blue. Plus, his right arm lay in a plaster cast. 'Who's done this? Inflicted, hell-bent violence. It's deplorable.'

Alfred explained he'd fallen on the pavement and whacked his head on the kerb.

'Come on,' I snapped! 'Someone's done you in! Can't kid us.'

He gazed straight. Eyes forlorn. 'Perhaps! Though. It's my fault. Made a few enemies round these parts. But what's done is done… I'm the one lying here.'

A few moments later, he pawed up his nightshirt. 'Here. Press a fist into me chest.'

I declined the offer. Alfred insisted. As he thought for some peculiar reason—if forced hard, a damaged chest would heal, and the swelling reduced. This was ludicrous! And typical of Alfred's medical knowledge. Thus, I dismissed it with contempt!

I tried to reason sense. 'Look! Let's get the doctor. He's the expert! Because Victoria's worried sick. Don't think she can't take much more.'

Alfred went enraged. 'No! I can treat myself. Thanks. We don't need some idiot lecturing us, inspecting me for sport. I know everything regarding medicine. Better than any doctor.'

I despaired. 'You're a stubborn bastard. Right! There's no point quarrelling. I'm through!' Abruptly, I stormed from the bedroom.

Alfred erupted. 'Yeah, that's right, mate! Piss off! Piss off with the damn doctor. You and all the other do-gooders. Bloody arseholes. Stink to high hell! Hear me… stink!' He lifted a vodka bottle and threw it at the wall.

****

During the next few days, Alfred's health deteriorated, and there were indications his mental state had cracked.

I wanted out! To escape to a new flat, but that "Damn promise" I made to Alfred meant I had to care for Victoria until he recovered.

But it was while both of us ate breakfast one morning, that we heard him 'Reciting Shakespeare.' Surprising. As I presumed, he had no acting ambitions.

Alfred then banged on the ceiling. Stating giant snakes crawled upon the walls.

When I arrived in the bedroom, the old man waved his arms and threw things everywhere. He said a massive snake was dividing within the ceiling, and then spiders, loads of them, had manifested. He begged us to snatch his cane and beat them into the cracks on the floorboards. I saw nothing. However, Alfred was adamant! So, I ran to the wardrobe, grabbed his Victorian cane, and dragged it across the walls and ceiling.

Medicine bottles and other items scattered underfoot. Yet, after a few minutes, I'd fended off this imaginary snake and its spider counterparts.

Victoria panicked. 'What's going on?' she shrieked. She repeated the phrase. 'What's happening? Stephen! Tell me!!!'

'For *Christ's sake*,' I yelled. 'Cool it!'

Eventually, I replaced the cane and stepped toward Alfred. His eyes squinting. Face twitching. And body shaking with distress.

I tried to reassure him. 'There's nothing there anymore. Scared the snake and bashed the spiders into oblivion. See for yourself.' I pointed at the white-washed walls.

Alfred opened his glazed eyes—before struggling to a higher position. Gradually a deathlike shroud set on his features and mood. And he said he wanted to die.

'Here! Don't give up the ghost!' I said, incensed. 'Understand. The grim reaper can wait his turn!'

'Stevy,' he croaked. 'There's one more—'

'—Listen, *fella!*' I finished. 'Victoria needs ya! What'd you think will happen? If you die? Her spirit would break.'

Alfred rubbed his chest. 'I'll try. Oh! How's it come to this!? To end up in such a pitiful, pathetic way. WHY?'

'Doesn't take rocket science. Refused hospital care. Won't see a doctor. Now,' I added with a warning. 'I'm a young dude. Got a life. So, won't be here forever. Will I.'

Alfred shrugged. 'Yeah, sorry, boy! Being a pain in the arse. An all that.'

We chatted and joked until he drifted off to sleep. Then I quietly exited.

'Alfred's calm. Snoozing,' I said to Victoria. 'Talked sense, and reasoned with him. Should be okay for the day.'

She smiled. 'Do hope he can pull through.' I nodded in agreement. Then made it clear if Alfred got worse, she would telephone the doctor, even if he argued against it. Finally, for added security, I gave my work phone number.

Therefore, we bid goodbye, and I left the house.

The events with Alfred over the last few days had caused unwanted pressure. I knew I needed stiff drinks at the pub that evening to relieve stress. Liven the mood. And remove the pit in the stomach sensation.

Chapter Five

It was now ten-thirty in the evening. I enjoyed drinks with work friends and felt cheerful.

Thomas and his wife stood near the bar. At the same time, sixties music echoed within, accompanied by singing, the sound of darts hitting dartboards, and bellowing laughter: it brought an atmosphere of calm to refresh my weary mind.

Thomas placed a hand on my shoulder. 'Hey, Stephen. Stay the night. We've got a spare room. Take it from a friend. Get away from that old couple. Ain't healthy. They'd send me mad. Come on! What do you reckon?'

I declined the kind offer, smiled and said I'd see him tomorrow. Then began walking to Alfred's and Victoria's abode.

A few steps into the journey, a *man* bumped rudely into me. I stopped and asked for an apology. But instead, he spun and eyed us like a rabid wolf. The guy was Trevor the Barman. I recognised him immediately.

'How's the old fool? Suffering! Enjoying pain?' he said without pity.

I stood still for a second and felt tempted to smack him in the mouth, but I did not feel in the mood for a fight, so I walked on.

Then a thought preyed on us. Could this be Alfred's mystery attacker? I would ask the old man later.

Meanwhile, at the house, Victoria was in the kitchen cleaning.

Alfred banged on the ceiling, asking for her to come upstairs.

Victoria groaned as her hip ached. She slowly clambered the staircase, pushed ajar the bedroom door and asked, 'what was wrong?' The old man mumbled and said, 'he had never felt so ill.' Next, he instructed Victoria to turn him onto his back as his whole body ached. She did this, feeling the strain, then asked, 'if he wanted anything to drink?'

But he told her his lemonade would suffice.

Victoria tidied the room and exited the bedroom. Alfred's pale, thin face stared wearily at the clock as he drifted in and out of consciousness.

Then he struggled for breath. Thus, Alfred knew death neared. Fear overcame him, and he whispered aloud, 'I'm sorry... so remorseful for what I've... done in life. Please, *God,* Don't want to die like—' Suddenly, Alfred clutched his chest, moaned in pain, and died.

He then experienced a death *vision.* At that moment, he had a mental picture of him and Victoria as children, holding hands, strolling through a beautiful garden, smelling the fresh, beautiful air. The scent from the flowers and a ray of wonderful sunshine lit the entire landscape; it had a dreamy feel. A minute later, Victoria halted.

'Cousin, why you stopped?' asked Alfred.

She immediately waved goodbye and continued in another direction.

'Victoria! Victoria, don't go!' His words were useless as she carried on into the yellow-coloured horizon. Alfred felt alone and hurriedly ran after her, but she had vanished.

Suddenly, the atmosphere changed—darkened and went oppressive. Alfred glanced nervously; two aggressive wolf-like dogs came at him.

Then explosions in the sky expanded like fire, and, to his horror, a head emerged from the ground.

Alfred shocked-still. The head changed. Solidifying. Fleshy tones gradually formed into the features of Trevor the Barman—the man responsible for his premature death. The body arose from the earth ahead. It carried a big club, and its face contorted with hate.

The old man turned and fled, screaming. Next, strange blackbirds more significant than crows swooped in the awe-inspiring amber sky—enlightening behind the apparition. Then Trevor trudged closer—before releasing a hideous laugh.

The old man stumbled. Fell onto the grassy ground, but instead of landing flat, he passed through the surface. He began a descent. It was dark, and voices and cries erupted.

'Help', he cried. 'Victoria! Stevy, please!' Then a whirling sensation pulled him to glorious lights. A window mysteriously opened in the darkness, and Alfred saw Victoria ascending the staircase.

'Hey!' he screamed, arms outstretched. 'I'm alive, Victoria! Here! Watch… *MEEEEEEEEEEE*?'

His cousin entered the bedroom and froze. Alfred's lifeless body lay on the bed. Immediately she screamed, 'No! Don't be dead. NO!'

Suddenly, a blistering flash, an explosive bang and Alfred vanished into the bright light of infinity, away from this world and into the next.

Victoria rested. Put her head in her wrinkly hands and sobbed.

****

I approached the house when suddenly a flash of orange sparks hit us. I shivered before an invisible punch struck my shoulder.

A blue *mist* manifested. Next, a flash of light dazzled, then vanished. I jolted and felt numb to the core.

At that moment, I knew Alfred was dead. I cannot explain this but sensed it. Perchance, I was psychic.

I hurried onward and noticed Victoria distraught by the house. We looked at each other, and she broke down. I realised Alfred had given up the ghost.

****

On Thursday, a week after his death, I attended the funeral. Victoria and a friend were the only other mourners in attendance.

It was a dull, miserable day with the rain hitting the small chapel roof.

I glanced solemnly at the casket and then at Victoria, who remained quiet and drawn, her friend giving support. The vicar opened his prayer book and lifted his head from a bowed position.

'May we sing the hymn, "Death is no End"'.

I listened but did not sing. However, Victoria sang with sorrow in her voice.

After the brief service, Victoria, her friend, and I trailed the wooden coffin, carried by pallbearers and arrived at a deep grave.

Next, they lowered the coffin with little dignity alongside other coffins stacked in the burial hole.

The vicar opened his bible and narrated a passage. 'Though I walk through the shadow of death. I will feel no evil. Believe in God. For he is the life and is the resurrection.'

During the vicar's sermon, I thought about many things. So this is how Alfred ends up? After all his life and adventures. The eccentric guy had pessimistic views of anything religious, but he had hoped that there might be 'something' after the cessation of physical life.

What with his belief in ghosts and spiritual matters. There has got to be something after this, or has there?

I dug into my pocket and removed a piece of paper. It had the line. *Time Is The Essence. For The Rest Of My Duties* scrawled in ink.

I stared. Remembering this was the 'phrase' that Alfred would use to indicate he'd survived death.

I put the paper into my damp pocket and glimpsed at the grave. The vicar finished his address, and this was the signal for the gravediggers to start their morbid job—shovelling earth into the grave.

Victoria and I then paced unhurriedly towards a waiting car.

The gravediggers sniggered as they did their deed. I heard a few of their nasty jokes regarding the buried coffins, and I glared with disgust.

One gravedigger laughed and began mocking the dead. Finally, his glazed eyes met mine. 'Problem boy?'

'No, not really,' I replied. So I carried on before yelling, 'You think it funny to laugh? Do ya!? Well, just remember! You'll end up in a hole one day. No one's *immortal,* my friend!'

****

A year later, tragedy followed. Victoria had a fall while cleaning the house and died a few days later of pneumonia.

I think she lost the desire to live after her cousin's death. So, my *promise* to Alfred was at an end, and I was free of its terms.

I would now enter the wide world, preparing for life's next adventure.

Little did I know that the name Alfred and the proof of 'life after death' would return to haunt me many years later.

PART TWO

I progressed through the years and decades of the 1960s, 1970s, and to the present point of time, 1985. My life went through many phases; I suppose this is part of the learning process, which, for some unknown reason, defines our course of existence.

After the death of Alfred and later Victoria, I moved on. With my Army career finished, I found the concept of civilian life and work a struggle.

I left my job as a warehouse driver and went to Newcastle to see what I could try next.

First, of course, there were drugs that I experimented with. Their use endemic in those days. But I found the concept of smoking grass, experimenting with magic mushrooms, doing barbiturates, and inevitably LSD an unsatisfying distraction. What was the point? If I wanted to get out of my face, a bottle of Jack Daniels whiskey would suffice. At least it wasn't illegal.

At the end of the 1960s, I still seemed no nearer deciding what I wanted to do.

So, I travelled from Newcastle and went to Royston in 1974, a year of outlandish fashion, the three-day week—because of strikes and novelty fads.

After a brief courtship, I met and married my first wife, Jacqueline, in 1975. We aquatinted through friends and at first everything seemed fine.

However, problems ensued. I did not want children—the reason—an unpleasant childhood experience.

For me, the death of my natural father in Africa reinforced the notion. His place then taken by a thuggish stepfather.

A selfish attitude regarding this and other matters ended my marriage to Jacqueline. We stayed together for only two years before a divorce was finalised. Unfortunately, the *financial repercussions* of this escapade cost money, and the ex-wife got half of everything I possessed, including the house. I'd no time to mope around, though, and swiftly got myself together.

During my time with Jacqueline, the subject of electronics entered my life and became an unusual hobby. So, with that in mind, I went to college to learn the skill in-depth—anything to improve career prospects.

After a few years, I gained relevant qualifications and obtained a well-paid job in this field.

Subsequently came the beginning of the 1980s and a second marriage to Maria. Everything now seemed *perfect*.

However, I became intrigued by spiritualism and the paranormal.

I must admit I had never taken an interest in the subjects. Yet, they stayed in the back of my mind.

Then, in early 1981, my mother died. This event affected me as it would for any other grieving relative. I felt numb and weepy during the funeral and months afterwards, but thankfully the grief subsided, and I returned to a usual way of life.

One night, after looking through documents and searching for legal papers regarding my mother's estate and her 'Last Will and Testament', I found a scrap of brown paper in a plastic sleeve. The words inked on it were:

Time Is The Essence. For The Rest Of My Duties.

That was the phrase the old man Alfred asked me to write before his death. It'd show that if he made contact from beyond the grave in some form or another, it would prove *him*, and only *him*, had come through.

Maybe because of this and other things, I consulted a couple of Spiritualist Mediums. I wondered if any truthful information would be forthcoming. Unfortunately, this proved pointless, as the responses and answers they gave were vague and wrong. This matter caused an abrupt end to interest in the paranormal field.

In early 1984, Maria and I moved to a lovely semi-detached

house in the village of Oakley, Herefordshire. Due to Maria's requests, we acquired a couple of pets, a boxer dog, Rex, and a cat, Tiger.

Over the years, I amassed a wide selection of electronic equipment, mainly because of my job at the electronic company.

Everything seemed perfect. My hopes and confidences were premature indeed.

This would now be a good point to continue the story's second instalment.

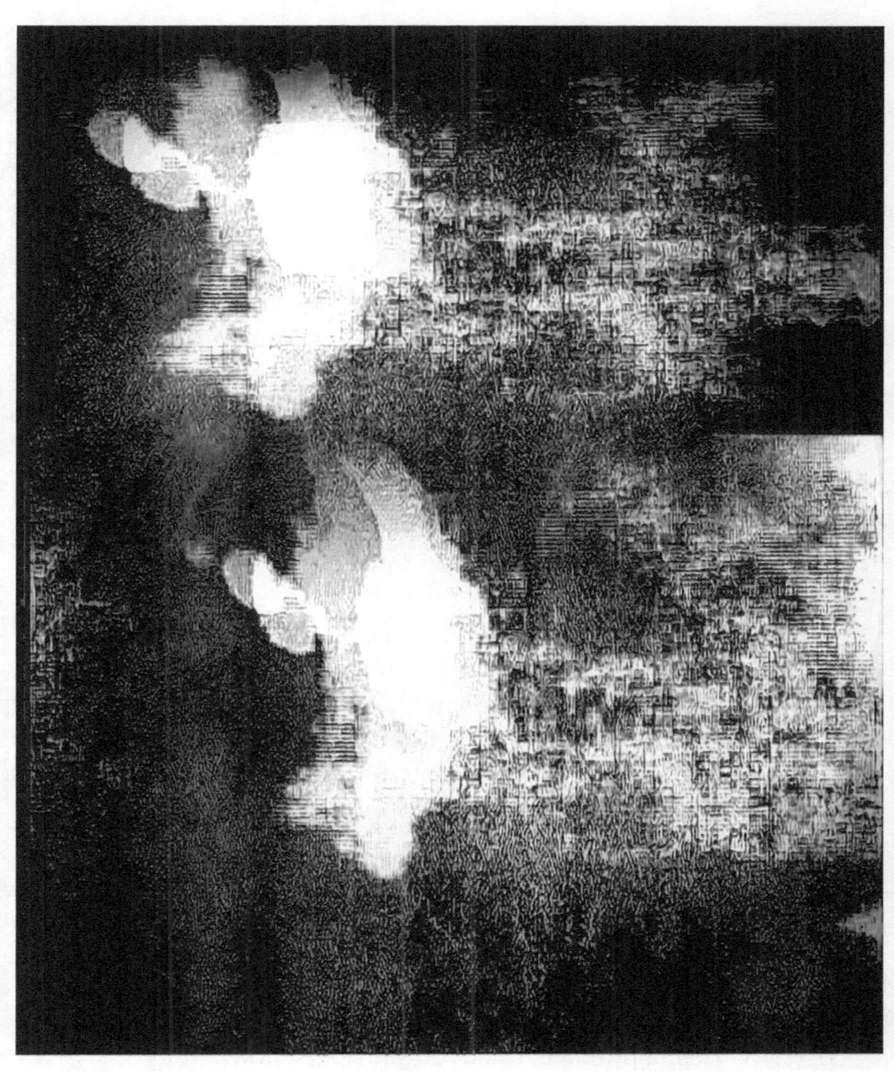

SPIRITS MANIFESTING ON TELEVISION SCREENS

Chapter Six

My age had unfortunately accumulated another twenty years. I was forty-five, with many unflattering ailments.

I now lived at the height of yuppies and wealth, which had merged into the Thatcher Revolution: The year 1985.

I'd worked as an electronic engineer for three years. The video and entertainment industry had exploded, and I'd gained lots of expertise in this sort of repair and building of commercial devices. But I'm afraid fortune would change.

Mr Bains, the boss, ushered me into the office; his manner was curt and abrupt. 'Your services are longer required!' Next, he gave a letter of *termination* of employment.

I glanced, stunned. 'You mean after all these years? The sack?!' Bains explained the company had transferred operations to the Far East. The simple facts meant that poorer and more experienced people were breaking the mould in this field of electronics. They were in abundance. Also, they worked for peanuts: my colleagues and I could never achieve this absurd ethic.

I slammed a fist hard on his desk and angrily dismissed his motives. 'Don't give me that! I'll tell you the reason. Never mind qualifications. Loyalty. The workforce there are slaves! Dirt cheap! You pay them a pittance, to cut corners. Arsehole!'

My boss stepped aside. 'Get lost, Stephen! Be on your way! You're no longer part of this company.'

I countered. 'Bullshit! Money! That's all it's down to! Thatcher's Britain stinks. Everything's for profit! Hear me!?'

Bains extended a hand to calm matters, but it was hopeless. The writing lay on the wall. I knew I'd lost my job. Become a member of an exclusive club, joining three million people languishing on the dole. Before I exited, I kicked one of Bains' chairs and slammed the door furiously.

Outside in town, I wandered aimlessly, feeling sad. Next, I stepped onto the road and nearly got hit by a car. I jumped— holding hands aloft in apology.

The car driver leaned from his side window, clenching a fist. 'Stupid idiot! Watch where're going.' His car then sped off.

I gave him the *V* sign and raged, 'Same to you! WANKER!' This caused dirty looks from a passer-by.

I trudged on, and the local library seemed inviting. I gazed at my digital watch. Then entered the establishment.

Inside, I idled time and realised another job had to be on the cards.

I glanced at the business section. Then, a book seized my attention. Its title: *How To Set Up Your Own Business With Government Funding.*

I know the title sounded cheesy, but I removed this piece of literature and flicked through several pages.

'Mmm! Seems interesting. Perchance. It'll stoke ideas. Work-wise, I mean.'

As I turned, I bumped into a ragged, smelly tramp. He dropped the paperback he held while ogling with a spaced-out expression.

Then he uttered slurred sentences. 'Here! Knocked me on purpose.' He spat on the floor—gashed teeth. And wildness transpired within the eyes.

My nose twitched as he stank. Next, the tramp threatened me. 'Come on, son. I'm pissed! Psychotic. Ready for all challenges. Y'know! I've got the power to destroy anyone. With remote viewing—*Eh*! What'd you think of that?'

'Yeah! Jus' like Uri Geller. Who bends spoons?' I stiffened and continued. 'Now! Beat it! No time for low *lifes*. I swear, I'll punch ya lights out!'

A couple of individuals motioned their heads and nudged one another.

The tramp and I shoved and brawled. Then, lastly, we squared up to each other to continue our rowdy fight.

I threw a right hook. And a left punch. Luckily, both missed. Otherwise, I would have been hauled down to the police station for assault.

A librarian who gave me the eye rushed to the scene and told us to calm it.

Abruptly, she ordered the tramp to her side. 'William! Refrain from nonsense!' She beckoned. And reluctantly, he followed.

After regaining composure, I trod on something. I glanced at the floor and noticed the tramp's book. I pawed it to my face, and the title triggered an inner question. A question that hadn't arisen in years.

Breakthrough An Amazing Experiment with Electronics To Contact Voices from the Dead. 'The dead and electronics,' I thought aloud. 'What on earth can this mean?' I read a few pages, drawing attention to various electronic terms and diagrams. The illustrations seemed simple for someone with the right knowledge to grasp.

I added this book to the other and hurried to the receptionist, who stamped 'return dates' on the inside covers.

About four o'clock, I drove my silver Rover car into the driveway. I heard Rex, the boxer dog, barking, which he usually did when vehicles approached the house.

I exited the car. Locked the doors. Then I carried my items—before using the worn front door key to let me in.

Rex appeared at the entrance—jumping, panting, licking his paws, before breaking wind like a fire dragon.

'*Hiya* boy! Alright,' I said while avoiding lumps of saliva that oozed from his jaws. 'Maria! You about? I'm home, honey.'

My wife busied in the kitchen, preparing a pan of stew. 'Just a moment,' she replied. Maria entered the scene and planted a kiss on the cheek. 'Good day?' Briefly, a cold sensation turned into sickness. My eyes could not withhold lies. Subsequently, I went sunken and sad. Maria seemed concerned. 'What the matter?'

I sighed. And explained the events of the day had left me jobless. 'As it goes. Take this straight! I'm a new member of the unemployment community. Fired! Today. The boss got rid.'

'What! A joke? Ain't it?'

'Afraid not!'

Maria was infuriated and yelled, 'Terrific! Now! What we gonna do? Can't live off the money I earn as a care assistant... can we? *Christ* almighty!'

Rex bolted upstairs due to the argument, disturbing Tiger, Maria's cat. Tersely, he meowed and descended the stairs, nearly tripping us up.

'Wretched animal!' I scolded. 'A haven for fleas. And useless mouse catcher! Take that! GITFACE!' I kicked his backside, and Tiger hissed. Yet, he took revenge by spraying along the wall.

'Cut it out! Leave him! *LEAVE HIMMMMM*!!!' shrieked Maria. 'Jus' head to the lounge. Watch television. *Chrissakes*! There's enough grief to contend with.' Then she disappeared into the kitchen.

I punched the wall. Cast grievance aside—and ignored the cat. Next, I entered the living room with agitation.

I sat in an armchair and pondered. 'I'll find a way of escaping this mess,' I uttered as I placed a finger on quivering lips. 'There are always folks who want TVs and video players repaired. It's the in-thing. I mustn't worry.'

God knows what's happened to the country? The only reason the firm wanted us gone was for profit! Let's call it the "Far East effect." The workforce labours for nothing less than a bed and hot meal. Sweatshop pay! Anyway, that's what I call it. Loyalty counts for nothing.' I grumbled. Held the television remote control and flicked through a few channels. I relaxed, but suddenly the sound of cracking emanated from the kitchen.

'Maria. What you broke!'

'Oh! Piss off!' A brief silence transpired before she exploded with other expletives. Accompanied by the scrape from an ashcan and brush.

My temper goaded me to counterattack. *Go on, Stephen. Give her what for!* However, I thought better of it. Thus, I pressed the volume button on the television remote.

While I gazed at birds chirping at the windowsill, the harsh sound of tv static erupted, and a flash of light dragged attention to Channel Eight—broadcasting a discussion program. Its subject deviated on Spiritualism and various methods of contacting the deceased.

A man in the audience grabbed the microphone from the host and started expressing opinions.

'I'm not questioning the ability to contact the dead,' he remarked. 'I'm analysing the methods!'

The audience fired into a frenzy, and rowdy ideas joined like fighting cockerels when these viewpoints clashed.

A boisterous man arose and stabbed a finger at one guest, a Medium—well, that's what it had on the caption.

'I speak! As a president! As a scientist. Who's studied Electronic Voice Phenomenon for decades?'

A few jeers carried from the audience. I perked with interest. *That book I got from the library focused on this subject,* I thought.

Within the cries from the spectators, the man continued. 'The experiments of Konstantin Raudive. Documented! Stated in his book, *Breakthrough*... is scientific proof. We can find a way through the realms of electronic ingenuity. To contact a realm. A dimension. That's invisible to the human senses. And cannot be explained with rational thought.'

The Psychic-Medium, named Dorothy, spoke in disapproval.

'The methods you're suggesting—I'm not disputing! However, it's the dimension you're contacting. It languishes on the lower levels. Earthbound entities. Demons! And evil spirits lurk there. There'll come through. And to you, sir. Heed this warning! They will. They can take you over!' The surrounding crowd exploded into mocking laughter, and ferocious insults ensued.

'*Mmm.*' I thought. 'So, this is what's getting the crowd's goat. According to intellectuals. There could be a method to penetrate a ghostly dimension using electronic equipment. Invisible and inaudible. However, people in the Spiritualist community dismiss the process as naïve and dangerous.'

Suddenly, a shout carried out. 'Be a love, Stephen. Give us a hand with dinner!' The smell of Maria's chicken stew stirred my appetite, so I agreed.

I switched On the video machine—to record the discussion programme, as its subject was intriguing. Therefore, I'd mentally digest the rest of its potential—and scientific examples—later.

At eight o'clock that evening, Maria hurried to work. Before she left, I said we'd discuss ideas on job prospects tomorrow.

I relaxed on the bulky sofa in the lounge. Switched On the video player and scrutinised the television programme about communication with the dead.

The subject seemed advanced and varied. It showed clips of Liam T Nelson, who claimed he'd built a machine to make two-way conversation with the dead a possibility.

Next, a televised segment of Nelson unveiling his invention to a packed London Press Conference. June 1979 occurred. And I bore witness to the demonstration.

A certain Patrick O Brennen, an electronic engineer and Medium, had contacted a Dr Moore. A man who'd died in 1931. I watched with excitement as video recordings from Patrick O Brennen talking with his Electronic Ghost appeared. He had built a Spiricom device to achieve contact—and several electronic diagrams sketched in precise detail showed instructions on how to construct similar machines. But unfortunately, the Press Conference descended into chaos as reporters heckled Liam T Nelson and O Brennen on the whole subject. O Brennen sat stony-faced as certain journalists asked awkward questions.

One of them called the whole thing: "A cock and bull pretentious fraud." At that moment, I switched the television Off and sat in silence.

Even though clouded by distrust at what members of the press said regarding Liam T Nelson and Patrick O Brennen, I cast this prejudice aside. And excitement swelled within. I genuinely believed this could be a way to contact loved ones who had passed to the Other Side.

Any person. Using an ingenious electronic device. With controlled experiments. Could witness how the personalities of the deceased energise? Transform. And ultimately return to the world of the living?

Various Spiritualist Mediums have confirmed this by stating transformation occurs after physical clinical death.

Chapter Seven

Over the coming weeks, I spent ages in the upstairs workshop. Attempting to build a machine that would enable two-way communication with the dead to become a reality.

I'd got many technical diagrams from unique books and articles on 'Electronic Voice Phenomenon.' As well as complicated literature about this 'Spiricom machine' that Liam T Nelson had been successful with.

Maria, unsurprisingly, was at her wit's end because of money problems. And furious with my obnoxious behaviour, so, unfortunately, we rowed frequently due to dwindling finances and Mortgage Repayments.

She'd stormed out twice in the last week. But marital problems held no concern. Because finally, tonight, over much toil and tears, I seemed near—or ready enough to test the electronic device I'd constructed. I hoped it would work. Then make me famous and wealthy.

A few minutes transpired—I glanced from the book, *Breakthrough* and wiped my sweaty brow.

The book's paragraphs and technical jargon thrilled us. It had drawn me to E.V.P. Like a drug addict wanting a fix.

I'd noted various methods, detailed by scientists, on how we could decipher the afterlife through electronic means. Mediate with it. As if making a phone call to a relative.

So now! I stood ready. The assembly of a Diode-receiving device completed. I soldered two wires to a five-ohms-circuit while placing a two-watt capacitor near the On-Off switch. After fiddling with cables, I wanted to see if this apparatus functioned.

I heaved the large, reddish-brown metal-encased object upright. My view drilled into it. Next, it began ticking like a bomb while positioned on the reinforced workshop desk.

Wires and coffee-stained papers lay on the floor. My feet twitched. Eyes widening. Then I pushed the plug into the wall socket and rested in the office chair.

I waited. Subsequently, I flicked the big yellow switch, and glowing sphere shapes from the device flashed erratically, as did the lighting within the workshop.

I electrified with excitement—enthused with total awe. The Diode device went mad. Crazy! With sparking power. The excitement taxed breaths and tightened the stomach.

Then suddenly. And in a flurry of electrical power, it erupted with deafening radio, white noise bursts. I clapped in pleasure. 'Bloody hell! Done it! Amazing! The thing's alive!'

I connected an extensive reel-to-reel tape system beside the Diode device. Also, I fed an audio wire to the tape recorder. Next, I leant to the wave scope monitor and switched it On.

The green screen illuminated with wavy line patterns flickering across like content goldfish.

With all this hand-built equipment prepared, I delved into the book, *Breakthrough* and Liam T Nelson's literature on the Spiricom device. I took a deep, controlled breath while relaying quotations from the books.

According to the documentation by Konstantin Raudive from his book Breakthrough, there appear, or so he claims, transmission stations that connect the two worlds with ours. Thus, we can contact this apparent dimension of the transcendental world of the deceased with proper care.

I now began the first experiment. This unknown science needed exploration. And I was the explorer—a man on a mission to find this world of ghosts.

I pressed the button on the tape recorder and stated the time and date. The digital clock flashed 8.24 p.m.

It was the 29th of March 1985. I 'addressed' the self-styled Radio Phoenix station. It existed in the world of the unseen like a beacon. I pawed headphones into my ears and held a microphone close. So that breath warmed its metal mesh. Then, with expectation, I tried for first contact. 'This is Stephen Reid. Radio Phoenix! Can I receive a communication? Respond. Please?'

Nothing happened! Nevertheless, I tried again. 'Reid here calling Phoenix! Can I receive any response? Any communications?'

This session went on for the next forty-five minutes. I kept repeating the same question but got no audible reply.

I removed the headphones, banging them on the table in frustration.

I did not want to believe it, but it seemed I'd been a fool! A fool to my own senses. I should've been sceptical. Cynical about Electronic Voice Phenomenon.

Consequently, I'd probably wasted weeks on a stupid practical joke.

However, I bit my lip—stiffened resolve. And with determination pulsating through my veins, I realised I wouldn't be stopped. Electronic Voice Phenomenon was pushing me, controlling me, forcing us to ignore niggling *doubts*. Yet, nothing could prevent me from continuing with this scientific pursuit.

I understood that persistence must prevail. Because before my very eyes, I'd watched Liam T Nelson's Spiricom machine animate. Like an intelligent robot, and this robot contained a deceased individual's personality.

'*Give it up*!' I thought. '*Never!* Not before trying another relevant avenue. I gotta be doing something wrong. That's the problem.'

This intriguing subject has captivated and perplexed my whole being.

I paused the tape machine with renewed energy, double-checking to see if it'd logged any voices. Then I checked the Diode device. It made a quiet electrical bleep, confirming it still functioned.

Thirty minutes passed when I played the tape again, but to my dismay, I heard nothing. The recording was blank! And remained on its factory designated silence.

Outside the workshop, Rex arose from his wicker basket near the stairs. He scratched, then nudged the door ajar. The dog whimpered. I figured I'd disturbed him.

A bark followed before he crept onto the scene. I glanced behind and fumed, 'What the hell! Do you want? Give us a break, Rex. Crikey?'

I stood, enraged at the intrusion. Next, I slammed the door. Then, after sitting, I decided I'd try the experiment one more time.

'If there are no paranormal manifestations,' I uttered quietly. 'Then possibly, I'll admit defeat! And so, if that be the case. I'll regard the book "Breakthrough and the science of Electronic Voice Phenomenon and Spiricom as complete fables."'

I reset all the equipment and placed the black headphones on, squeezing their two synthetic speaker cushions tight against my greasy ears.

For the last time, I directed tough questions at the Diode machine. 'This is Stephen Reid. Calling Radio Phoenix. Please respond?' I shook my head in frustration. 'Come on! Dammit! For *God's* sake! *WORKKKKKK*!' I tried again and demanded in a robust tone. 'Reid here. Phoenix! C'mon! Can I receive a Commu—?'

Rex released a couple of barks, interrupting the process, then stared aloft. Alert-like.

'Rex,' I said, puzzled, 'What's wrong?'

Suddenly, a strange humming noise emanated from the Diode machine speakers, and the level indicators flickered. I gazed around the room with expectation; the oscilloscope went crazy while the audio level needles on the tape machine hit the maximum.

I rose from the chair and removed the headphones. Expectations pumping furiously.

Then a whispering robotic hissing 'voice' manifested through the speakers—audible and strong. I struggled to grasp what could be happening. The words spoke phonetically, pausing. Next, after each phrase, the audibility increased! Intensified! Rex crouched on the floor, shaking and snarling. His brown hair was rigid, brought on by fear.

I assumed something other than the dog lurked in the room. Instantly, hairs on the neck went static when a voice uttered a mishmash of foreign languages, followed by guttural breathing.

'This is creepy! What's occurring?' I whispered.

A few orange flashes sparked from unique positions near the electronic equipment, creating mystical interference, which disrupted the tape recorder speed.

A loud knock at the window on the right-hand side made the senses solidify.

At that moment, a 'voice' spoke with clarity. 'I am Mellissa,' it said. 'Contact's established, Reid. I am the Mediator!' A brief silence transpired before it continued. 'Turn the voltage selector. Mellissa, will clasp that creative hand!'

Suddenly, the precious silver ring on my finger gently dislodged and vanished.

I jumped with excitement. The room vibrated. Shuddered. So, I swiftly stuck my right hand on the Diode machine and asked a question. 'Who are you? What are you! A ghost?'

My body shivered. Humming noises peaked. Then disbelief enveloped us.

Abruptly, another voice interceded, male or neutral in origin. At that point, with slurred tones, it announced, 'You've been chosen!'

I went shocked. Taxed breaths drew static sparks. And rapidly, the sparks multiplied. Congregated. More and more, before a group of voices whispering and speaking weird languages emitted from the Diode device.

I touched the supernatural box. A bright flash dazzled! Accompanied by a horrendous bang that sent me spinning backwards into the wall.

Rex barked and snarled and began growling with nervous *eyes* and quivering jaws. After that, the room became eerily quiet, except for the sound of the tape machine.

I rose from the floor. Waiting. Thinking. Observing. With trepidation, I paced cautiously to the Diode device and tape appliance.

I checked the tapes expectantly—hands trembling, hoping something documented.

Thankfully, and to my relief, everything had been recorded perfectly.

I wonder who Mellissa is? First, I read pages from the book *Breakthrough* and other relevant information but found no connection. Then, however, I noticed Konstantin Raudive had contacted someone titled 'Spidola', who acted as a mediator on behalf of the ethereal world of the inner dimension—and the name 'Mellissa' was also mentioned briefly.

Could this spirit be acting as a mediator? Which I'd somehow contacted?

'Success!' I yelled. 'Must've done it.' With authority and pride, I clenched my fist and shouted uncontrollably. 'BRING IT ON *SPIRITSSSSSSSSS!!!'*

Excitement coursed through my veins. Until Rex disrupted the exhilaration, he would not stop scratching the door, desperate to escape. Therefore, I nodded. Creaked it ajar, and Rex bolted down the staircase.

I checked the Diode device and other gadgets and switched all the equipment off. Then stepped from the workshop and firmly shut the door.

Later that night, I lay in bed with Maria. I was moaning and turning—finding it tough to sleep. However, somehow, I lapsed into the world of rest and had a weird, bizarre dream.

I stared through the living room window; a dark shadowy outline from a female greeted my vision before disappearing.

I then noticed a dozen or more people scattered everywhere. Because of their reclining position and lack of movement, I realised they were undoubtedly dead. They resembled a collection of marble statues in a Greek museum. Their faces were grey, eye sockets empty and dark, and features etched in sorrow and pain.

Hissing noises ensured, and I glided through the living room window. I came to a halt as the cry from a ghost changed to whispers. And then! I graced amongst them.

I stifled a breath. Then, suddenly, life entered the bodies. They began jostling and bashing against us.

I barged against one and cast the rest aside. Then they all began fading like an early morning fog.

I squinted my eyes to double-check this event before all dematerialised from the scene.

In their place, I witnessed two familiar people sitting on immense chairs. One, my birth father, killed fighting in Africa— and Alfred, the old man who died twenty years earlier—for some inexplicable reason.

With nervousness, I hastened nearer. 'Father. That you?' I asked, trance-like. 'Never got the chance to say goodbye?' He scowled. Withdrew a pistol and fired it into the heavens. In the expanding gun smoke, flags from Britain's African colonies flared in flames, and I witnessed visions of soldiers on the battlefield slumped upon destroyed tanks and burning planes.

Next, I turned toward Alfred. 'I'm confused. Where have all the statue-like figures gone? Is this a dream?' I uttered.

Before Alfred could answer, my father arose and vanished into a dazzling fire.

Then I faced the old guy alone. I asked the same question about 'where the bodies had gone?' He nodded and replied, 'They're coming to your tranquil house, Stephen. To play with radios. Toy with technology. And drag you to *HELLLLLLLLLLLLL!!!*'

I shocked-still! I tried asking another question but couldn't speak. A thick blue mist surrounded us, and I saw clammy hands yellow and black with decomposition, clutching and scratching.

Alfred laughed and mocked like a crazed sick hyena. I gritted teeth, hands curled into fists, and I wanted to beat him to a pulp for scaring us. Subsequently, I approached, squaring up to the guy. Nevertheless, I struggled for breath and only managed a timid yell.

In an instant, I awoke in bed, drenched in sweat. Shaking. Twitching. Panting. 'Damn it! Shit! Can't sleep again.'

Maria snored, rolled to the side, and groaned.

I shrugged, exited the Queen-sized bed quietly and went downstairs.

When I entered the living room, the smell of flowers hung in the air. I saw the ginger striped Tiger, Maria's cat, lying on the armchair. I stroked him, then stared at the oval patio window—the same one I'd dreamed about.

The moonlight night awakened a piece of nostalgia, while outdoors in the darkness, the wind made the trees rustle as if listening to fateful tunes.

'My father and Alfred,' I thought aloud. 'Had various dreams about him since his death. Yet, that's the first time I've seen Alfred appear alongside.'

Moreover, it certainly wasn't a dream. It was a nightmare! A terrible nightmare. Because something didn't add up, it was like Alfred had an evil twin brother. Goading! Tormenting. If something dreadful awaited on the horizon.'

Five minutes transpired. I felt unnerved and depressed. I twisted from the window and glanced at the keyboard, positioned in the corner by the antique cabinet. A small blue painted china doll given as a gift by my mother rested on a glass shelf.

I decided I would perform a song on the keyboard. The musical instrument I'd owned for a lifetime.

I sat on the stool like Mozart and performed a soothing melody. A melody—written years ago in my reckless youth.

As I ran fingers over the keys and played the keyboard with pleasure, I disturbed Maria. She wondered why her husband decided to create musical songs this time of night?

Maria arose—wrapped an oriental patterned dressing gown around her before leaving the bedroom.

I'd been performing a multitude of songs, getting into full flow, when Maria whistled—resting against the doorway, listening. I stopped and apologised for waking her.

She smiled and strolled nearer. Her blue eyes reflected the light like precious crystals.

Then, Maria placed her head on my shoulder and kissed us softly while the scent of her perfume stirred love and happiness.

'Never heard those songs,' she said. 'They were beautiful. Take it. Couldn't sleep? Why not? What's the matter?'

'I dunno. Suppose… stuff and nonsense, Maria,' I said. 'Worry. Memories from bygone eras. Regrets. To name but a few. However. Been deliberating,' I added. 'On everything that happens in a lifetime.'

"Are our pathways echoes? Do we realise that life's journey dissolves like dreams we endure in sleep? We dash through life scratching a living, absorbing the knocks it offers along the way, and we hardly ever ponder the hours. Let alone the days or years or the people we leave behind. The many formats that events create have such an impounding effect on our emotions that I wish sometimes I could be excluded from the consequences of this merry-go-round of pain, tears, fear, and love."

'I understand, for I've lost a mother. A father… and childhood pets,' said Maria. 'Yet life weaves a mysterious path. And we're dragged end to end. Accepting its fate…. But destiny brought us together. Which is important?' she added. 'For love is our strength. And our strength is our bond. Which can never be broken.' And with that, she kissed me on the lips, and my heart raced with yearning love. I held her hand. 'Just as philosophical on life as I.'

Maria nodded in agreement. 'Come! Return to bed.'

'You go. I'll be there in a moment.'

She agreed—and exited.

I rose from the keyboard and edged to the window. Gazing in a profound, knowledgeable manner. I pondered about the experiment I'd started earlier and wondered if I could be sure contact had been established with the spirit world. This notion triggered a 'question.' Longing. Exploring. I speculated If I could interact with friends and relatives who died. Would this change the philosophy that dictated my scepticism concerning ghosts and religion? I knew I had to gather as much information as possible from this Mellissa entity. She was the critical link to the Electronic Voice Phenomenon experiments.

Perseverance had taken hold. It was a mentor. However, I had to be discreet. I wanted to be sure *I* could continue two-way communication with no technical issues. Perchance, another spirit would enter from the realms of radio noise. That would be incredible.

This electronic science was fascinating. Mesmerising! I wanted to take it to the extremes and give these top-notch scientists a run for their money.

So, on that thought, I exhaled wearily. Yawned and retired to bed.

Chapter Eight

A few days passed, and conversations with Mellissa, the electronic ghost, centred on various subjects. They were becoming defined and detailed.

Somehow, though, I kept the exchanges from this entity secret from Maria.

Nevertheless, grave issues had arisen because of unemployment and lack of money. Household finances teetered on the breadline. And I knew I had to get a job: Urgently

On Thursday morning, I chatted with Maria in the kitchen, the discussion deepened, and she fired suggestions. 'Plans today? Bills are rising. And we're behind with mortgage repayments? Already had a debt collector ring twice. Lousy cockroach.'

'Excellent turn of phrase, love.' I considered. Deliberated. 'I'll have a drive round. Visit guys with connections. See if they can lend a hand. Throw work in my direction.'

'You've given that same excuse for weeks,' she retorted. 'In heaven's name. Step to it. Use your nut. C'mon! Why don't you visit Gordon?'

I was puzzled. The name didn't ring a bell.

Maria's stare pointed. 'Y'know! The Gordon Parks guy. Was a colleague. From years ago. Had a reputation. A Romeo, by all accounts. Used to get the local women over the—'

'—I don't wish to know!' I finished.

Then suddenly. Gordon's name ignited memories. 'Ah! Now I recall. Bloody hell, haven't seen him in yonks. Wonder what he does now?'

'Opened a television repair centre. In town.' Maria passed yesterday's newspaper—detailing the shop advertisement, her face scowling like an angry teacher's.

So, on that action, I thought it best to heed advice before her patience snapped. Quickly, I glanced at the shop's address. Re-studied the local rag's opportunities and assured Maria I'd visit Gordon.

I kissed her on the cheek, rushed to the hallway and grabbed the car keys.

I coughed. Slipped on a sheepskin coat and exited. 'Maria! See ya later. All being well.'

My wife responded with a tirade of expletives.

Typical! I thought.

As her outburst faded, the fresh air smelt sweet, and I hastened to the car—a haven from the wrath of Maria.

Though, at that moment, the paranormal recordings I'd done the previous night burrowed into my mind and soul like a computer chip dictating orders. This ghostly subject consumed me. Drawing us further into its sphere of frequencies and spectral voices.

Yet, I had to concentrate on the present: A job! And a gut feeling told me that I'd strike lucky.

Later, while driving, a bastard in a Blue Capri began tailgating, which continued for a few minutes.

Suddenly, toots from the car's horn startled me! Before its wheels screeched and the thing overtook—the idiot driver resembled a crazed drunk.

Road rage boiled. I nearly exploded. Still, I wasn't in the mood for a race with an arsehole. So, I ignored the jerk! Maybe he'd kill himself with a bit of luck.

I regained composure. Then I noticed, to the left, a sign *written* in bold green letters. It was Gordon Parks' TV Repair Centre. Thus, I slowed the car and parked.

Gordon, by the look of things, had done well. The appearance of his business dazzled with sheer class.

I chuckled. And thought, *It'd be a pleasant surprise to meet again, after all these years.*

I examined a JVC Stereo Music Centre and a Betamax Video Recorder inside the premises. However, the prices were outrageous. There's no chance I could afford them!

At that point, I saw televisions. Monitors. Radios and video equipment. They all peppered the shelves—to entice customers.

A young spotty chap advanced. 'Excuse me, sir. Can I help?'

I guessed he was sixteen. So, I acted stern. 'Gordon here? Y'know. The boss. Proprietor?' The kid just stared. Unsure.

I persisted. 'Come on, lad. Tell him it's Stephen. Stephen Reid. We go back. A long way.'

'One moment. I will fetch him.' He headed into the rear, and murmurings shadowed. I twiddled fingers. Whistled. And waited with trepidation. Abruptly, the voices ceased.

When silence transpired, and before I could react, Gordon entered. He had mousy coloured hair swept from his brow, which disfavoured his vanity.

However, it had been eighteen years since I'd last set eyes on him.

I grinned. Gordon's features cheered. He flashed a smile and slapped his knee. 'Stephen!' he said applaudingly. 'Of all people! It's great! What a wonderful surprise!'

Instantly, we sealed our meeting with a handshake. 'All these years,' I said, thrilled. 'You've done well!'

'You bet!' he replied. 'Even though. I've struggled. Immensely. What with taxes and red tape. But we've made it through the worst. Shop's running. And awash with trade. Anyway,' he added warmly. 'How's you and Maria? Both keeping fine?'

I was hesitant. My mouth dried. 'Erm! Maria's okay. But, I'm afraid, old boy. A crisis is brewing.'

'Elaborate, mate?'

Tersely, the shop door jarred and in strolled a customer—his body odour reeking like unchanged pants.

Gordon asked Tony, the youngster I'd met, to deal with the guy.

Then, he escorted me to the back office, and we resumed the discussion in private.

At the house, Maria continued with the dull task of cleaning, with Rex being a nuisance. Tiger growled! And Meowed. *Cat wants to be fed?* she thought. She rose from the floor. Called his name, but there was no sign.

'Where's the blighter?' she uttered as she exited the kitchen and hit the living room. Her gaze darted to the four corners. Yet, all she saw was Rex panting by a chair.

Maria ascended the stairs. Paced the landing—searching, though still no sign of him.

A noise spread apart like thwacks from hands, and the workshop entrance *drew* attention. Then eyes. Mysterious eyes appeared before dissipating.

Maria witnessed the door creak open. It was unsettling and disturbing because I always kept the place locked whenever leaving the house for a time.

Devious noises peaked to a crescendo. Maria cast a worrying look. 'Tiger. You in there?' She trod cautiously. A slight chill brought concern. Then cries erupted—cracking the walls with thunderous anger.

Maria recognised the noises. They were Tiger's.

The cat was fighting something. Something unholy in the workshop. Therefore, without concern, Maria dashed through the entrance.

The scene which unveiled terrified her. Bated breaths sapped strength and froze her to the spot. Maria bit her lip and gnashed her teeth until one chipped.

Everything happened in slow motion. Tiger battled something.

Could it be another moggy? She thought.

That theory vanished when nothing visible manifested. Then without warning, the Diode Machine and tape recorder powered On.

Tiger's fury became like a torrent. Like angry rivers seeking souls. Maria threw a fist to her mouth and bit it until the flesh bleed. 'STOP IT!' she wailed in a cry packed with turmoil. 'In god's name! Stop this madness!' She tried to snatch him, but Tiger lashed out furiously. '*ARGHHHHHHHHH!!!*'

The cat tore from the room. Next, the Diode machine released a robotic-type laugh while its brownish-red metal box invented rapping knocks that timed to Maria's thumping pulse.

'Prepare for transmission,' hissed a voice. 'A transmission from ghosts.' The tape recorder ceased. And the room filled with an eerie silence.

Unexpectedly, everything went misty, cold. And the atmosphere electrified.

Maria witnessed a dark dungeon-type place filled with wailing people, moaning, and weeping. She felt faint. Dizzy. Her coordination failed. Then spiking fog manifested.

Suddenly! She was a child again, that same child with her favourite teddy bear resting on her knee.

Maria heard her mother read stories before everything faded into echoes.

The light dimmed. Darkened. And taught breaths taxed Maria's lungs. She tried to fight this attack. This vision. Anything to prevent its onslaught. But she couldn't. She trembled. And her trembling became uncontrollable when a crawling hand moved along the darkened wall with sinister intentions.

Maria remembered this precise moment from childhood. The night her older male cousin died. A man she despised. Who made her afraid? For he was evil. Had evil ways—thus, Maria had tried to banish these sickening memories forever.

However, this evil man had returned from the dead. His

sneaking hand shadowed the ceiling, then spread apart when the roar from a thousand rising ghosts turned into screams of regret.

Instantly a dark force arose and dragged the thing to the lower realms of the Astral Plane. The earthbound hell where all evil spirits reside.

Just as the vision appeared, it vanished, and everything returned to normal.

Maria shrugged perturbed and hurried to the Diode device, flicking through pages of literature positioned adjacent. The previous evening I'd read an article on contacting the dead and methods of building an alternative Spiricom machine.

Downstairs, smashing, squeals and howls pierced like a nauseating slaughterhouse. Rex and Tiger fought one another. 'Christ!' she cried as tresses of hair blinded her. 'Nuts! Everything is a shitstorm!' She threw the pages aside and exited.

In the lounge, whimpering ascended and held for a time before Maria arrived. She bore witness to Tiger tearing lumps from Rex. The cat was mad—like a caged, starved animal.

Maria 'screamed.' She darted to the kitchen. Fetched a steel broom while sounds from breaking ornaments in the lounge intensified—caused by the animal fight.

Maria tried to separate the pets with the broom. Finally, it succeeded when Rex freed himself and bolted out, knocking her to the ground.

She lay still to gather energy before blood trickled from her scratched arm onto the carpet.

She glanced aloft. Suddenly, to her horror, she came face to face with Tiger. He hissed and snarled as if possessed while blue mist distorted his features.

The doorbell rang! And re-echoed. But this did not affect the behaviour of Tiger, as his eyes widened and shape mutated.

Subsequently, the cat arched and released an ear-piercing shriek while gnawing into Maria's cheek. She cried as his canines drew blood.

The doorbell 'exploded' as the cat prepared to finish his task.

Maria squinted. Then rings from the phone meant someone on the line—and the rings sent the animal into a fit.

At that moment, the *picture* of Maria taking her wedding vows shattered from atop the television.

Tiger recovered, but terror enveloped Maria. He jumped past her and climbed the swaying velvet curtains.

Outside, a car approached. Its wheels spun on the slippery road, and 1980s music from 'Frankie Goes to Hollywood' blared on the stereo.

Maria panicked. Gasped. 'Tiger! The damn car. He's got no road sense.' She arose, dashed to the door, and released the catch. Rex watched—slouched upstairs, licking his wounds.

A Ford Blue Capri, driven by Craig, a drug dealer, approached.

'Jack! I'll settle the score tonight. We'll do the deal. Stick the cocaine. Shaft Cartwright. Then all be settled. Will cash out the pimps.' He laughed uncontrollably. 'This is what life's for. Grief! Goading the police! For kicks.' He laughed again. Recklessness thrilled. 'We live and love! And screw the law.'

His companion smiled. Then, through a smoky haze, he saw Tiger crouched. 'Hey! Do the cat! Dare ya!'

Craig leered. 'Yeah! Roadkill! HA! I'm in the mood!' He hit the accelerator.

Maria witnessed the unfolding event. She gazed left, and the car speeded past.

'Oh! No. My *God*!' she screamed. '*STOPPPPPPPPPPPP!!!!*' Brake pads on wheel discs screeched, and the vehicle skidded. A loud thud ensued. Birds scattered. But it was too late. The car had crushed the cat. He twitched his white paw and then died.

The car didn't stop and raced off. Its driver, Craig, shook his fist in triumph.

The phone continued ringing. And in a state of shock, Maria went inside. She removed the receiver and answered. 'Hello?' No answer. 'Stephen. That you?'

A voice filtered through. Robotic in manner. 'Tiger's here! Here with us!… *Cleopatra* hussy.'

'Pathetic sicko!' bawled Maria. 'Damn you! DAMN YOU!!! You hear me?' She smashed down the receiver.

Clutching her arm, Maria drew apart the nets and peered through the gap. She saw neighbours placing Tiger into a plastic bin liner, their faces flushed with dismay and sadness.

****

At Gordon's place, I enjoyed cigarettes and cups of coffee while discussing events that occurred over the decades.

Rude remarks transpired about Bains, my old employer. I pondered. Then a caffeine buzz from the coffee triggered inquiries, 'Any jobs going?'

Gordon said the shop was doing great, and he could use a guy for the repairs department.

With that, spirits lifted. And I felt relieved Gordon had hired us. The wage packet would ease the financial situation and reassure Maria. We cemented the deal with a backslap, and I exited.

Quickly, I hurried to the pub for a celebratory beer. However, I'd only graced the establishment a short time when I eavesdropped on pub regulars discussing a cat: Killed on the road, with a hysterical woman bewailing.

SHIT! Can't be Tiger? I thought.

Instinctively, I exited and drove to the house. However, when I pulled into the driveway, I noticed the curtains drawn and feared the worst.

I let myself in. 'Maria! Home, honey. Rough and ready. Where are you?' Then I shut the door.

'Having a bath,' she uttered from upstairs.

I entered the lounge. There! I saw broken ornaments on the floor, our wedding photo in pieces near the TV, and the carpet peppered with bloodstains. Thus, I searched for a reason to explain the mess.

Maria entered, wearing a dressing robe—her tear-stained eyes met mine with penetrating grief.

'What an earth's happened?'

'Tiger! Went berserk! Attacked everything. Now he's dead.' Maria fought her sobs mournfully.

I noticed Rex; he rested nearby with badly injured paws.

'I dare to ask this. But how'd he die?' I paced the lounge, detective-like.

'Crushed! By a frickin' car! He sat in the middle of the road. As if… he had a death wish. Tiger escaped,' added Maria, 'through the small window. Terrified! Y'know, Stephen. Something frightened him. Began in that workshop.' Maria removed a tissue and wiped her eyes. 'I felt weird. Confused! With edgy vibes when I entered. Like a bad LSD trip. The cat fled to the lounge. Then attacked us—during a violent fit.'

'Terrific!' I said, voice deepening. 'Do I need this or what?' I undid my shirt collar and loosened the tie. Next, I inspected the ornaments strewn, far and wide.

'Now! You're certain, Maria. The workshop triggered it?' An air of foreboding crossed my features.

'Yes, Stephen! Definitely! Eyes don't lie. Now you better believe me! Cat went berserk. Crazy. Fighting things unseen.'

I nodded in agreement.

Now I'd secured the workshop before leaving, I thought. *So how did it become unlocked? And how did the cat get in there?*

The experiments I'd conducted with the Diode device and the strange paranormal voices captured on tape concerned me. Surely there wasn't a connection? It's not that I was using an Ouija board or conducting a seance. The paranormal manifestations originated from transmission stations in the spirit world. Not from inside the house. Or perhaps things have changed?

I exhaled tiredly. 'Well! If it's any consolation, Maria. Secured a job. Gordon Parks hired us. Doing repairs and stuff. Now I'm part of his team.'

'That's something.'

After a tender hug, we cleaned the living room. Then the unpleasant task of burying Tiger awaited. A black sack containing him rested against the door.

I dug a hole by the fruit tree in the misty garden and sited the cat's favourite toy mouse close. I gave a goodbye kiss before completing the burial. The trickle of rain followed. So, I hurried from the morbid scene. First, however, I stopped to catch my breath. At that moment, I felt something prickle upon the neck.

I saw a reddish bird sit atop the fence. A violet glow surrounded its body—and it 'observed us studiously.'

More birds appeared—prior to them departing to a haunting tree. The glow of the moon, like a feral eye from a devious god, enlightened the tree's branches, making them come alive. Bewitching. Scary.

I shuddered. Carried the shovel and went into the house. There I comforted Maria.

We chatted, and she gave details about the car that struck Tiger. "A Blue Capri Sports:" Driven by evil bastards bereft of pity.

My conscious enraged. That same car hassled me earlier while driving to Gordon's place.

If I ever found the scumbag drivers, I swore they'd receive a proper hammering. It would be a great misfortune if I bumped into them.

We needed stiff drinks. I poured a Napoleon brandy while Maria settled for white rum. Hopefully, the alcohol would soften the blow from today's events.

Later, I went to the workshop. But I didn't flick the light switch.

First, murky darkness greeted me. Next, I noticed the oscilloscope flashing. Then, finally, L. E. D. lights on the tape machine blinked. I became puzzled, as all the equipment should be Off. But then I'd locked the door when I went out, and for an unknown reason, it unfastened with Maria alone in the house.

Interest brewed. I hurried to the devices. Switched On the fluorescent light and glanced at the floor. There! I noticed electronic tools disseminated, probably caused by the commotion with Tiger.

I studied the tape machine, and surprise thrilled within because another reel of tape lay inside—played halfway thru, with the microphone positioned studio-like. My gaze flicked at the Diode device. It remained stationary—had not budged, despite other objects out of position. 'Maria!' I yelled. 'Disturbed any stuff?! Y'know! The workshop's a mess?'

'No! Course not,' she replied. 'Anyway. Wish you'd frickin—'

I slammed the workshop door—silencing Maria's anger.
Gradually, I removed several electronic items from the floor.

I pressed a red button and watched reels of tape spin.

A right hand drew to my chin. Then I shrank into the chair, focusing on the indicators.

Unexpectedly, a burst of 'white radio noise' erupted. I tried to adjust the levels. Peculiar growls climaxed—resembling feral cats. The sound kept cutting. Flickering! With drop out interference.

I felt unsettled. Emotions enveloped. The animal noises on the recording were Tiger's. I made adjustments and heard Maria's distorted voice filtering within.

Abruptly, I switched the tape machine Off, as I didn't feel in the mood to listen.

Suddenly, and to my astonishment, a 'hideous whispering voice' emanated. Its words marked and audible levels high. I did not require headphones anymore as the voice came from the speakers beside the Diode machine—this had never happened. Also, the voice's pitch from the Diode machine thrilled unholy.

I took leave of wits. 'Can someone talk?' I asked. 'Directly? Do it! In a perfect way. Acknowledge! Listen. And reply to questions?'

Mellissa, the electronic ghost, responded. 'Hello, Stephen.' Its eerie hissing speech rising and falling. 'I stand inside the room… In the *Zimmer*!'

A worried expression surfaced. For the first time, it seemed possible that I could conduct a two-way conversation with this ghost with just the Diode machine. My heart thumped and thumped again.

I shivered. 'Who are you?' I queried. 'What are you? You've said during earlier experiments. Your voice emanates from a transmission station. Positioned in the spirit realm. And not from the house. Why the change? How are you now able to give timed answers—to questions?'

'The link is now strong. Prevailing! I'm ready to enter the earthbound plane.' Mellissa stalled, then continued. 'You have opened a doorway. An astral doorway. It's given access! From the ascending city of the dead.'

My whole body electrified with excitement.

Abruptly, a male voice interjected. 'I fight the cat. He does not like!'

Mellissa re-entered. Unnerving. Rhythmic. 'There is someone here. Who wishes to communicate... Reid?'

I felt nervous. 'Who. Erh! Who is it?'

A brief silence ensued. 'Stevy boy. It is I. Alfred!'

I threw a severe glance. 'Alfred! That really you? Have ya survived death?'

'Smoke the pipe. Love tobacco,' he rasped. 'Can have anything I like. Stephen, I see you. Can touch that face. Be at your side! Dig this room. Groovy! In it! Get me drift. Ha! Ha! Ha!'

'So! You're in the room. How can that be? Aren't you speaking from...erm. Some kind of spirit transmission station?'

Tersely, his manner and attitude altered. 'Can't I even get through? You flaming bastard. Despicable slimy skunk!'

'Repeat! I don't understand. Why the change in tone?'

'I hated... Victoria!'

It paused, then he, or whatever it was, uttered something regarding his lifetime appearance. However, the description given was nonsense. He labelled himself tall and well-built. In his 40s. With thick brown hair. Finally, he said he'd died in a traffic accident.

This declaration was false. As the Alfred, I knew died from complications after an assault. Plus, comments on Victoria, his cousin, made little sense, as he adored her. Mind you. They had barmy debates and rows when I lived with them.

Another male voice with threatening tones entered. 'We inhabit the house, Reid. Travel within its walls. Its heart!' I ignored this voice and directed another question at the Alfred personality. Suffice to say; his reply was rubbish.

My challenges annoyed him, and he thundered, 'Stephen! Stupid shit. Listen! I speak. You're deaf! Can't hear my words. Diabolical fool!'

I rebuffed angrily. 'You are not Alfred. Only an imposter.'

His voice faded, and the Mellissa personality retorted. 'I'm the *Devil!* Here we love not a soul. Can pick a fight! I come to the house. I will possess you… Like the possession of the pigs. The ones from Israel. Before Jesus Christ cast them out!' It screamed these sentences in a way a lunatic might babble if trapped in a mental asylum. Next, a hissing laugh fired from the other would-be antagonist, Alfred.

I'd had enough and wanted the experiment finished. So, mentally drained, I barked. 'I've no interest. In your kind, anymore.'

Mellissa countered. 'Do not turn the Diode apparatus off. It will cease communications. And weaken the link. Understand, Stephen? UNDERSTAND? There is no such thing as *time* here. I see the future. As prophecy is our gift. And so, that same gift is our power! Despicable man! Never disrespect. Never display naivety!!!'

I shook my head. Then switched the machine Off. A faint robotic-sounding scream sounded, and a horrific laugh trailed before everything went silent.

I began trembling—as if someone had stepped upon my grave while unsettling thoughts deviated.

I touched the Diode device; it felt icy cold. So quickly, I

removed a pen and wrote notes on a paper sheet.

I pondered, reflected and deliberated about the sphere or realm where the voices emanated from.

A two-way conversation had now been achieved, just like Liam T Nelson and Patrick O Brennen's Spiricom device. But the queries I asked Alfred confused me. I graciously asked relevant questions to begin with, but his comments back were totally out of character and incorrect. However, they justified I'd encountered someone else in a discarnate unseen world. Moreover, the Mellissa character preyed on my mind, as it had a hostile approach building, especially when I dismissed the character impersonating Alfred. The guy I knew from twenty-odd years ago.

I exhaled wearily, feeling perturbed. Then exited the workshop and locked the door.

A couple of nights later, Maria and I rested in bed. The portable television broadcasted the movie 'Blithe Spirit', starring Rex Harrison. Ironically, it had been Alfred's favourite.

A mighty wind wailed, making the bedroom windows rattle, and outdoors, the trees swayed as if deathly phantoms travelled amongst them.

Nevertheless, I continued reading books about Spiricom and Electronic Voice Phenomenon, then noted one article.

Electronic Voice Phenomena And
Spiricom: Fact Or Fantasy

During the 1960s, a Latvian scientist/psychologist living in West Germany named Dr Konstantin Raudive developed a technique using tape machines, diodes, and radios to contact deceased people. Over those years, Raudive amassed thousands of recorded phrases claiming to be from people who, when alive—knew the experimenter Dr Konstantin Raudive. Many emanate scientists listened to his recordings and were baffled and unable to verify where these voices came from. Konstantin Raudive died in 1975, leaving a legacy for other researchers to carry on his work.

How did Raudive become known to the broader world?

The Inaudible Made Audible was Konstantin Raudive's original German-edition of E.V.P. experiments he documented. This book caught the attention of UK publisher 'Colin Smythe' in 1969, who subsequently made available an English-language version: *Breakthrough*—this gave Raudive's research more significant publicity. Peter Bander wrote a preface in the book about how he first heard a strange voice. The voice said: "Mach die Tur auf"—German for "Open the door". Bander immediately knew the voice was from his dead mother. Bander became convinced of the genuine nature of the Electronic Voice Phenomenon and wrote a book titled.

Carry On Talking How Dead Are The Voices

Twelve years later, Liam T Nelson unveiled a radical new way to contact the dead, aided by an electronic psychic engineer Patrick O Brennen. The year was 1979, and they had designed a weird electronic machine called 'Spiricom,' short for spirit communication—this enabled O Brennen to have a two-way conversation with a Dr Moore, who died in 1958. Much controversy and media interest followed, only to dissipate when other scientists and experimenters could not replicate the results Liam T Nelson and Patrick O Brennen achieved.

A 1990 article published in a newspaper disputed the true nature of the entities that spoke on tape, televisions, computers, and other electronic devices. The points raised were these really people who had died and wished to make contact? Or were they clever malevolent ghosts fooling the researchers communicating with them?

I took stock, trying to digest all I had read. Then my attention briefly restored to the present.

I'd not been in the workshop for days. Too afraid. Plus, irrational fears, combined with a reflective imagination, created all manner of weird conversations and morbid images.

Maria's usual bottle of Bacardi rested by the phone on a small table, and with biting malice, she drank another glass.

I tut-tutted. This triggered a drunken altercation. 'Haven't said much. What's the matter?' rasped Maria.

I ignored her and continued reading. Maria went restless. Forceful. At that moment, the bedside lamp flashed. I put the book down and answered. 'Come on, Maria. What's the problem! Trying to concentrate.'

The movie 'Blithe Spirit' peaked in the background. Then Maria exploded. 'Stephen. For Christ's sake! Speak to me. Don't be difficult. What's that wretched book you're reading? All-pervading. I suppose?' Immediately she snatched it.

'Here! Give it back!'

Maria ignored us and flicked through a few pages before her face furrowed with concern. 'What's this bullshit!? Electronic communication with the dead! Mediums! Life after death. I don't believe it. You gone completely mad! Well. Stephen. Give me a straight answer!'

'Maria. You're naïve. Subject's complicated. Just interested. That's all.'

Suddenly the cream-coloured telephone rang, interrupting the quarrel. Maria removed the receiver. 'Hello.' Silence greeted her. 'Hello! Who the hell is this?' Still silence.

A burst of electricity erupted. Her grasp spread apart. 'DAMMIT! There's something wrong! Someone's screwing with the goddamn phones!' Maria rubbed her palm against the duvet. 'Stephen,' she uttered. 'That's the second time—some prankster's called. I'm sick of it!'

Abruptly, a disturbing memory returned. Prior to the Blue Capri that killed Tiger—the phone rang. When Maria answered, a strange neutral robotic voice 'addressed her' with menace: *Your cat is here with us now!*

Maria prepared to relay this when Rex barked.

'Great!' I scolded. 'Dog's started. I'll have to deal with the bugger!' I arose from bed and paced to the doorway.

On the landing, the light dimmed. I tried the switch, but nothing happened. Thus, I walked tentatively onward.

Rex stopped barking. A 'massive bang' exploded, causing the house to shudder. The television in the bedroom fell from the table as if abused by an invisible fiend.

Maria dashed to the scene—angrily berating, 'Stephen! What's going on? Dog barks. Then nothing. Crazy!'

Suspicion crept upon me. The unfolding events stirred dread.

The barking restarted. However, it came from the workshop. Maria stifled a gasp. I bit my lip and gestured, 'Wait here, love! I'll deal with it!'

Shortly, blue gunk seeped from the walls—followed by the sound of a loud click! The door unlocked, and Rex's barking intensified. I couldn't fathom it! Was I right in the head? Were my eyes and ears employing tricks? I thought this whole drama nonsense.

I threw caution aside and bashed open the door. There! I stared into the darkness. 'Rex! You in here?'

No reply! Only unnerving silence. The tape recorder powered On, and, to my dismay, the Diode machine followed suit. I thought it best to escape.

Abruptly came a massive slap! Something struck my jaw. I shivered. Froze! An enormous flash ensued, and static electricity surrounded us. I forced fists to my ears but stumbled—falling into the workshop.

Maria 'shouted.' The door slammed shut. She tried to force the thing ajar, but with no success.

I lay still and felt disorientated. Within the workshop, darkness enveloped, except for L.E.D. glows that flickered on the tape machine and Diode device.

A strange electrical charge packed the room with revolting odours while Maria screamed—thumped, and banged at the door in terror.

I adjusted my head. 'Show yourself! If not, be human?'

Mellissa, in her mysterious *voice,* responded. 'Make a good impression of a dog. Don't I, Stephen? How do you like being in the dark? Enjoy it. Here with us? *We trick the demons. Goad priests for kicks?*' Her accent turned thick and threatening. Then a multitude of blue flashes dispersed.

I struggled aloft. A bright shadow flashed past, causing all hair on the neck to stiffen. Next, I felt a sensation *touch* the right-hand side of my cheek.

Maria frantically twisted and jerked the handle. 'Stephen! Please. The door won't budge.'

In the room, I heard a familiar ghostly voice. 'Reid, it is I. Alfred. Y'know the old geyser. In the room now. Don't need the damn machine to make contact. Or to spy. Say! Saw your wife in the shower the other night. You're a lucky guy. I'd like to—'

'—BEAT IT!!! You filthy bastard!' I finished with a roar. 'YER HEAR *MEEEEEEEE!*'

Maria entered, and I made for the exit at that moment, leaving palpable fear languishing in the horrifying workshop.

Maria went emotional—distressed. And I, badly shaken, shaken to the core by the entire experience.

'Something's depraved in there,' sobbed Maria? 'Tiger knew. Now it's happened again.'

I steadied. Then went firm. 'Now! No one enters the room! Until I know what's going on.'

Without warning, Rex bolted onto the scene and barked fervently.

Suddenly scratching noises spread apart, moving along the floorboards—running inside the attic. This tipped Maria over the edge. Lack of sleep. Alcohol. And grief turned into a hideous shriek '*ARGGGHHHH!!!*' Shaking overwhelmed her. Her face snowed white. Then a glance! A gaze fixated! Vacant eyes with nothing behind. Then, when the shriek faded, she went for us— rubbing and clawing. A rising knee followed, impacting my groin. '*CHRISTTTTTT! MARIAAAAA!*'

Somehow, I forced her to the floor. She lay jolting. Resting on her back. Floods of tears became a torrent. Yet, still, she lashed out with bloodstained hands.

'GET A GRIP! MARIA! PLEASEEEEE! *STOP THISSSSS!!!*' She exhaled an exhausted sigh at that split moment, and her eyes peeled shut. The trails from her tears brought a lump to the throat. I buried my head in her chest, for I loved her so much.

I considered. Then I helped Maria to a seated position—wrapping tender arms around her—hugging her tight.

I glared at the workshop—anger and fury propelled within. I wanted to confront the dreadful things that now lurked in there.

****

Hours later, the Blue Capri, Tiger's executioner—drew to a stop on the deserted *Shackleton Road*, eighteen miles from town. The car's headlights remained on, waiting for a signal. 'Park here, Stuart. Nothing fancy. Cartwright's due! Ten minutes.'

'Still don't like this?' said Roy.

'Cool it! Everything's arranged. The deal will be completed. Shortly.' Gradually, bright lights like that from a lorry approached, appearing through the rear window.

'That should be him! Leave this to me,' said Stuart. 'I bargain hard. Take no prisoners.'

At that moment, the bright lights vanished, and the Blue Capri's headlamps exploded. The two partners grimaced! Panicked and threw fists at their eyes.

Suddenly, mundane claustrophobic darkness encased the car, smearing the passenger windows with thick smog. Then sensations erupted. Terrible. Horrific. Agonising in their power.

'What the hell! Shit!?' screamed Roy. 'C'mon! Cartwright's double-crossed us. Listen? We've been set up all along!'

Stuart thumped the dashboard and tried the ignition key, but it seared into his flesh. Instantly, his fingers flared with fire and skin peeled from the bone. '*ARGHHHHHHHHHHHH!!!*'

Roy tried the passenger door. Rapidly, a violent electrical shock shot up his arm. Then it snapped with a sickening break. The forearm bones dangling apart. '*NOOOOOOOO!!!*'

Roy begged. Pleaded. Cried! As the car shook forcefully—knocking side to side.

Claw-like scratches tore into Stuart's chest, ripping his designer sweatshirt and blood spewed from gaping wounds. He struggled. Fought. Anything to defend himself from the invisible attack.

Suddenly, orange mist accompanied by electrical humming manifested. It transformed into a human shape, resembling an older man. Roy turned. Instantly, a slicing grip took his neck. 'My throat. Don't kill us!'

A yellowish leather claw panned with deliberate movements, creating a momentary paralysis: then a click! And Roy's neck snapped. His friend, Stuart, bore witness to the deep lesions! Inflicted by a hideous knife.

Two strange *Occult Symbols* burnt on Stuart's chest. He traced "Save Us" with a bloodstained finger on the windscreen in terror.

Next, he released a dreadful cry, a final death rattle and then died.

After completing its macabre task, the unearthly orange mist clarified and smiled with disturbing indifference.

This evil thing was Alfred. The same entity who had presented himself to me.

It remained still for a moment, then vanished—ready for its next course of action.

Chapter Nine

After the events in the workshop and the death of Tiger, I sent Maria to her sisters for relief, and recuperation, to soothe her mental state.

During her absence—dealings in the house became settled. No more strange voices or noises manifested. But, mind you, I always had a fear something prowled the home thru the dead of night. Thus, Rex slept at the end of the bed for companionship.

When time allowed, I fixed a sturdy lock on the workshop door. Also, I ensured and double-checked all the equipment remained Off, especially the Diode machine.

The main trip switch that fed power to the workshop was carefully re-routed to a fuse box under the staircase.

When Maria returned, she seemed tranquil. Therefore, the following day, I felt relieved when I left for work.

****

I completed repairs on a damaged television and dropped a screwdriver into a box.

I glanced at the clock before noticing Gordon safeguarding a video recorder. He smiled and suggested we take a well-earned break.

I sipped coffee—and drilled a question. 'Mate. Gotta discuss something. Important.'

'Sure,' he replied. 'Let's take a seat. Right! I'm all attention.'

'This might sound weird,' I began. 'Y'know, coming from me. But, try to be objective. Have an open mind.'

'No problem.'

'Ever heard of Konstantin Raudive? Liam T Nelson?' I lit a cigarette. 'And Patrick O Brennen. Or read their books?' I took another drag on the cigarette to kill the tension.

'Yeah! Remember Patrick O Brennen. Built a machine. And talked to a cranky ghost—always fascinated, on how he achieved that.'

'Well!' My voice tightened. 'Believe this! I've achieved similar results. Constructed. And assembled my own Diode machine.'

'Wow! Stephen. You're off track. In the deep end. No one! No one ever matched "Patrick O Brennen's" results.' Gordon considered. 'I recognise your drift, though. The subject, I mean. I recall—various stages in the seventies. The guy, "Konstantin Raudive!" Pioneered experiments with tape machines, radios, and Psycho-phones. To contact the dead. But I never knew what the hell a Psycho-phone was. Suppose, jus' another electronic device he used in research.'

'Indeed,' I remarked. 'E.V.P. experiments! I've done them—used methods from books. Wanna hear? Y'know? The results?'

Abruptly, I removed two cassette tapes and waved them ahead. Gordon hesitated. Then gave a nod in agreement. My friend inserted one tape into a recorder and listened.

The tape slowed when its spools slipped before a click! Then automation occurred, and the cassette settled. Gradually, an unearthly humming filtered within the speaker.

The robotic voice of Mellissa manifested, followed by eerie chat from Alfred.

Gordon squinted. Attempting to rationalise these ghostly conversations. The tape continued for twenty minutes, then ceased with an audible pop!

My friend sat in stony silence. Digesting what he'd heard, as these unholy robotic voices remained in his head for ages.

'What do you reckon?'

Gordon pondered. And severity crossed his features. 'Dunno. There's definitely something! But I'm baffled by the content.'

'See! Supernatural voices live! Exist on tape.'

'Be that as it may,' began Gordon. 'But you're talking ghosts, for heaven's sake. Where's the goddamn proof? Crikey! It could've been a crackpot using C.B. radios. Or a Walkie-Talkie nut! Perchance, a radio-frequency hacker.' His brow furrowed. 'Nevertheless. Take qualified advice. If you're getting signals! From wherever these voices transmit. Cut the experiments! Immediately!'

I gripped his shirt. 'Can't! Too involved! It's like a drug. Anyone! With an ounce of desire. And armed with audio equipment. Can contact a dimension from where discarnate spirits speak? We can communicate! To the other side. Electronically! And perceive the realm they inhabit.'

'Stephen!' reiterated Gordon. 'Leave this bullshit alone! I had a mate. Who dabbled with the Ouija board! Ended up sectioned. In a psychiatric institution. His mental health—ruined.'

'Don't make comparisons,' I snapped. 'This is radical science. A new frontier! That I must explore. So! Save the lecture on ghosts and poltergeists. They can't harm! Understand.'

It was on that last 'word' I faltered. The "Nothing can harm me quote" rested uneasily.

I believed in ghosts for the first time and wondered about my involvement with E.V.P., especially after the workshop's events. And I knew I could not dismiss Gordon's concerns. Thus, I dragged hard on a cigarette, exhaled, and became perturbed.

'Everything okay. Home wise. Is Maria fine? You've gone pale.'

'She's bearing up,' I countered.

'Come on,' shot Gordon, 'Speak the truth! Anything to do with this crap you're dabbling in?'

I knew I had to tell him. 'Take an apology. You're right. Look!

Ever since I conducted experiments.' Grief grew within my sentence. 'There's been incidents. Disturbances—I can't explain. Tiger died. You know that?'

Gordon acknowledged.

'Now Rex is acting nuts. The other night. I saw something *in* the workshop. My gut reaction! It was sinister. Not of this earth. Talked into the ear. So, what with that? And the stress it's caused. Maria's in a state. I wish I could end this entire episode.' I tut-tutted. 'Oh! This is crazy!' I finished the rest of my cigarette and bowed—exhausted. Then, I ranted incoherently about the Diode machine.

Gordon suggested I leave the tapes. He said he'd check various textbooks on the E.V.P. subject. And run advanced tests.

'Steady pal. Don't fret,' he said reassuringly. 'I'll chat with someone. Who's wise. Got expertise. On this paranormal topic.' He slapped us on the shoulder.

We heard 'shouts.' Tony, the young shop assistant, entered. 'There's a Mr Benson outside. Returned his television. Wants to make a complaint. Said he couldn't watch the "Evil Dead" film. Something to do with shoddy work. Performed on the video player.'

'Bloody cheek!' raged Gordon. 'I'll deal with the burke! Told him not to modify the vertical switch. Probably fused the tube!'

****

Gordon rested in solitude. Thinking. Contemplating. And chewing gum to pass the time in the shop.

Yet again, he listened to the tapes. He placed fingers on his mouth square-like and thought on. Then an idea sprang to mind.

He would telephone Dr Andreas Neilson. A distinguished Spiricom and Electronic Voice Phenomenon expert.

Gordon removed the receiver and made a phone call. Dr Neilson answered and listened with interest. Subsequently, after forceful persuasion, he agreed to fax several pages on the subject.

A wait ensued. Gordon tapped his fingers on the desk. Then a pointed glare hit the Fax Machine as it printed pages. He pawed the sheets into a pile and brushed aside wires and capacitors. Next, he sited the information-packed pages atop the counter and began reading avidly.

TV Heaven ITC
In Pursuit of Images

Are the pictures seen on televisions and computer screens a modern-day mirror of Spirit Photographs taken over a hundred years ago?

This is a new science that has strengthened in popularity. The spirits first captured decades earlier on reel-to-reel-tapes by Konstantin Raudive are starting a new skill by revealing themselves in portrait from the Other Side. A ghost using E.V.P. contacted Paul and Stephanie Taylor, a British couple. And advised them to disconnect their television aerial and switch to the analogue, white-noise mush: an occurrence where there are no broadcasting television signals.

The Taylors set up a video camera, pointed it at their television screen and began recording. When they rerun the footage, they observed several entities—one a deceased relative. As time passed, they developed two-way communication with the Spirit World by using television sets, computers, and fax machines.

Konstantin Raudive, Alfred Einstein, British explorer Sir Richard Burton and Thomas Edison have apparently manifested.

The Taylors also captured one intriguing image of a girl. They identified her as 'Alison Spinks.' Who died in 1874 and lived in Scotland. She had crossed over from the Astral-Timestream and wished to contact the experimenters; her existence ratified through the video screen mush.

The word Astral Timestream means Spirit Station, a location on the Other Side where ghost-technicians transmit their physical identities. Their spirits emerge from this eerie place and into our electronic audio-visual world.

A female spirit communicator, Sophia, is working on the Other Side, or Timestream—its official title, to assist the Taylors with these impressive pictures.

Some sceptics have alleged that the Taylors' pictures are fake and manufactured.

But one photo emerged. It was of the late Donna Steel. Founder of the E.V.P. association, Canada. Her face was youthful. Clear in clarity, even though she died in her seventies. She looked about 25 to 30, which equates to spiritualist theories about your appearance in the world of spirit. However, there was something I found perturbing. Her right hand's configuration had eight fingers instead of five.

Dravis Zenta, a retired Swiss firefighter, has received similar results as the Taylors—capturing an image of his deceased wife from a television screen.

To conclude. Obviously, some of these Spirit Pictures could be fake, but I cannot explain with any scientific fact if others are genuine. When I attempted experiments, I never achieved the same results by pointing a video camera at a television—with no signal—and replaying the videotape. Instead, I only received eye ache due to glaring at a screen full of electronic interference.

In addition, there is uncertainty. Unsettling. Unexplained. I'm still not sure from what source these spirit pictures emerge. They could be genuine spirit people or copycat entities using an individual's weak point—any trick to engage in a conversation with the living.

Dr Andreas Neilson. October 1983

Gordon exhaled. Unfastened a drawer and removed a small paperback detailing another scientist's research into Electronic Voice Phenomenon. He shrank into his chair, poured a whiskey, drank, and then began reading.

Experiences in the Science of EVP, 1976. Mr Derek Crane

After conducting experiments, I achieved splendid results—the process took time, though. It did not happen overnight. So, I set up a recording session one night at 8.30 pm, as this was the best time to conduct experiments.

Seemingly, there are many transmitting stations on the Other Side used by spirits to cross the bridge from 'their dimension' to ours to make contact.

At first, when I started, I tuned a radio to the 'white noise' between stations, got my Pioneer tape recorder with a microphone plugged in, placed it near the speaker of the radio and began contact.

For three weeks, I addressed if any friends from the Other Side would like to contact us. Then, after playing back the tape and listening to the recording session with my headphones, I heard nothing, only the hiss of radio noise.

But on the twenty-fifth day of trying, I listened again and heard a voice in the 'white noise' interference addressing me: *'TALK TO US?'* I was astonished by the results, and as the weeks progressed, I got many EVP messages, some saying: *'WE ARE IN THE ROOM.' 'I CAN SEE YOU.'* And others made comments about what I was doing during a recording session. Further messages I received were in German and other foreign languages, though, which I could not understand. This made it harder for me to respond. On another night—I'd been eating an apple before a recording session. When I played back the tape an hour or so later, I heard an EVP message reply: *'APPLE GIVE US A BIT. I'M FAMISHED!'*

The EVP phenomenon is something that I can't explain. And is a genuine science that cannot be dismissed. Even though I have talked to some psychic mediums, they have different views about the subject here in Europe.

Some have been positive, while others have explained you only get evil spirits entering, and other comments bordering on the extreme.

Konstantin Raudive's book 'Breakthrough', with numerous EVP quotes from the dictators Lenin, Stalin and Mussolini, may have influenced the psychic mediums in their opinions, especially when: the German Dictator Adolf Hitler seemed to manifest frequently.

According to Raudive, Hitler's documented comments still showed the same traits that characterized him on Earth: self-glorification (Megalomania). Various voice examples recorded by Raudive seemed to indicate that the dimension Hitler inhabits is some kind of hell.

Mediators

These are Spirit entities that help in the link-up process in EVP. If using the radiofrequency method, i.e. a radio tuned to 'white noise.' A number of transmission stations exist in the beyond. They are—Goethe Bridge—Kelpe, but the main one seems to be Radio Phoenix.
A highly respected EVP experimenter achieved some fantastic results with this method. His EVP messages received were on a par with Raudive's.

Gordon rested for a time, trying to rationalise all the written information he had digested. Finally, he glanced at the clock—it had stopped! Gordon panted. Eyes widening. The moment had frozen. Was it a sign? An omen of things yet to come?

Chapter Ten

At the house, Maria listened to classical music on the Hi-Fi. She relaxed on the sofa as the evening passed. Then, abruptly, the doorbell chimed, and Maria hurried to the door.

The next-door neighbour's wife, Carol, stood at the front entrance—holding a few vinyl records.

'How're things?' she began. 'Pulling through? Here! Brought a few L Ps. I thought they'd help. They're my favourites.'

Carol gave Maria the records and relayed news from a colleague running errands for the Police. 'Incidentally. Want some juicy information. Could be of interest.'

'What is it?' replied Maria.

'Know the *car*. That got Tiger.'

'Yeah. Those shitbags in the Blue Capri.'

'Apparently! For reasons unknown. Police found it parked down *Shackleton Road*. The driver and his companion… Dead as doornails. Trapped inside. However, there's a sting in the tail,' added Carol. 'Been informed. The police suspect both—were murdered by some maniac. Deep scratch marks littered one body. While the other sustained a broken neck. Head twisted all the way round. Finally, bloodstained lettering traced on the windscreen. The phrase said, *SAVE US*.'

'Done in! That's scary,' uttered Maria uneasily.

'I know. Crime scene's crawling with detectives.'

Maria shivered—disturbed. However, she composed herself. 'Fancy a coffee? Could do with company.'

The neighbour smiled and agreed to the warm invitation.

They drank their hot drinks and watched the News Broadcast. The announcer, without detailed info, confirmed the 'Murders'.

Then Maria and Carol gossiped on rumours doing rounds in the neighbourhood.

After an hour, Carol told Maria, 'If she didn't want to be alone. She'd be welcome next door.'

Maria was grateful but declined the offer. Thus, when they'd finished talking, Carol exited the house.

Earlier, *I'd* asked John and Carol to keep a watch on Maria while I was out. However, Carol had thrown a spanner into proceedings by repeating stuff about the murdered drivers from the Blue Capri.

I knew what had happened. And felt elated—such sweet revenge for poor Tiger.

Maria went to the kitchen for a glass of water, then returned to the living room. She read the titles of Carol's records and put one on the Hi-Fi. She settled in a luxury armchair, relaxed, and listened to the music's dulcet tones engulf the room before her eyelids shut and sleep enveloped.

A couple of hours later, the night darkness had thin beams from the Moon when it spayed upon the windows.

Maria blinked, then awoke—feeling relaxed.

Rex rested on the leather couch and panted. She thought it best to usher him to the garden.

When she rose, the phone rang. She flicked the light switch, hastened to a small table, and removed the receiver.

Suddenly, tension grew in the lounge. Thickening. Menacing. Perhaps the sound of the phone triggered something. However, Maria noticed the turntable spinning. The Hi-Fi had not stopped. The rotating plastic disc continued—the stylus-arm jerking—repeating endlessly on the empty groove of the record.

Maria yawned, flicked her hair, and placed the receiver to her ear. 'Hello,' she murmured, only silence transpired. Maria's lips dried. 'Hello. Anyone there?'

Instantly, a ghostly singing voice arose. Then, with audible echoes, it recited a name.

'....... *MARIA! MARIA. MARIA. MARIA.......!*'

'Who's that?' she asked.

A static click jarred against her cheek. Next, the line went dead. Maria gazed at the handset. She stared at the four corners of the room. Then, abruptly, the Hi-Fi emitted music, followed by green sparks tracing upon the stylus' arm.

Unexpectedly, and to her surprise, the Hi-Fi's power ceased, and the room was devoid of noise.

Before she could react, a 'voice' rising and falling from upstairs sang, 'Maria! Come. Play with us!'

Rex went alert. Barked, and the brown hair on his back pointed rigidly.

Maria heard the strange voice linger like a cry from a dream. Thus, she exited the lounge and stood at the bottom of the staircase. She peered into the oppressing darkness and pressed the landing switch.

Then, ascending the steps carefully, she drew nearer to the cry from this calling voice.

At the top of the landing, she headed to the workshop by the white painted staircase. First, she put her sensitive ear against the door. 'Can't hear a thing?' she thought in whispers. Next, she tried the handle, but it was stiff, locked and bolted.

Maria shrugged and paced the landing, arriving at the large square window—an older adult, his body enlightened by a 1950s streetlamp on the road, motioned at the house, catching her attention, and Maria gazed at him intently.

Suddenly, the older man halted! He turned, and his eyes met Maria's. The man wore a uniform similar to a German Nazi SS Officer's. Then people ran past, and he vanished in a bright glare.

Maria's feelings deepened. Nervousness grew. Then the keyboard downstairs conducted a tune. The notes resembled a 'perverse orchestral opera.'

Maria thought she heard footsteps and glanced over her shoulder. The old man from the road reappeared; the bottom half of his legs below the knee gone, enabling him to glide to the house. Then, abruptly, a ghostly hissing voice announced. 'WE ARE IN YOUR HOME!' Frightened and disorientated, Maria's senses couldn't grasp the words.

The old man, a ghost imitating Alfred, levitated laterally to the front of the house and its ghostly expression fastened at the window.

A loud bang rang out, and the house shuddered. The living room door slammed—trapping Rex.

Maria revolved clockwise in a mesmerizing state. Pointing a shrilled gaze at the window.

Then, and to her absolute horror, she came eyeball to eyeball with the entity. Its features were malformed—pressed hard at the window. Her *eyes* widened and enlarged with fear. Finally, the ghost's expression chalked white, and its mouth opened, revealing its contents.

Its slimy black tongue lolled and tongue-lashed a name: the name 'Alfred.' Maria shocked-still. Chest thrusting. Ears aching. Feet sweating. Maria couldn't move. She was paralysed—paralysed with terror. She wanted to scream. Oh! How to scream. But her voice held still.

The ghost turned evil. Hate twitching its jowl and appearance.

Rapidly, a dark, hooded figure appeared behind her before disappearing.

Maria felt a frosty breeze rifle her hair. Next, an aura of paranoia and unreality engulfed the scene.

Then the hands of the ghost reached through the glass and grasped Maria around the head. Its hands were yellow, grey and clammy—and covered in gut-wrenching fluid. Lastly, after a struggle, she broke free and screamed. 'NO! HELP *MEEEEEEEEEEEE!*'

I approached the house in the car and noticed Maria pressed against the landing window, bashing her hands.

I stamped on the brakes. The car skidded and screeched to a standstill. Unsure of events, I tried casually opening the driver's door.

Suddenly, an electronic buzzing encircled us. I threw fists to my ears. 'TURN IT OFF! I screamed. '*TURN IT OFFFFFFFF!!!*'

The central locking device activated—trapping me inside. I shook my head. Then the buzzing ceased.

I witnessed Maria's chilling anguish. I panicked. And observed a shaft of light hovering at the window opposite her.

I tried the driver's window. It was stuck fast! Wouldn't budge. I thumped the doors, head-butted the steering wheel and knew I had to do something. Anything, as Maria's life, hung in the balance.

Suddenly. There! I saw the steering lock. I hoisted it aloft and smashed one window. At that moment, the interior light exploded. Scratches covered my brow, but somehow, I struggled out of the vehicle and onto the grassy verge—shaken, with grazed elbows.

A shout erupted. Then John, the neighbour, exited his house.

I struggled. Bewailed. Screamed! 'For God's sake. Do something!'

'WHAT YOUR GAME!!!' he fumed.

On the landing, Maria was hysterical. Arms spreading apart. Frenzied panic on her face. 'Stephen! Help. *USSSSSSSS!*'

I dashed to the entrance. Tried the keys. Snap! The lock jammed. Maria 'screamed' and banged the window.

I twisted the damn key again, but to my horror, something had fastened the lock from inside.

My shaking hands went upward. 'NO! NO! DAMMIT! *DAMMITTTTTTTTTTTTTT!!!!*' Filled with rage, I shoulder barged the door.

John sprinted towards us. 'Stephen,' he uttered breathlessly. 'Your wife! Sounds like murder?'

'Think an intruder. Is in the house. Gotta break down the door!' John agreed and struck the wooden frame.

Rex howled furiously in the lounge, knocking chairs aside—chewing anything in view. Digesting carpet—tearing holes in furniture. Eating table legs as if they were bones. Crunching ornaments as if there were lumps of candy.

Carol, John's wife, stared from her bedroom window. Concern crossed her features—eyes widening with dismay.

My temper exploded. I kicked the door. Rammed it. Until cracks appeared before the wood divided, and splinter shafts sheared my leg.

'Come on! Come on!' I yelled. Everything was crazy. Adrenalin arose. My throat tightened. Then at that moment, I screamed as I'd never screamed before. It seemed an eternity when a blistering click split the heavens, and the lock gave way.

The door flung ajar, and John and I outlined as the moon's luminosity turned us evil within the doorway.

John grabbed a metal object from the floor and hurried to the back of the house.

I dashed upstairs. Heart pounding. Sweat pouring. My hands curled, and the rage in my voice bellowed. Roaring with a vengeance. 'Get away! You! Bastard. Stay away from my wife!'

Suddenly. There! I saw Maria. For a split second, I froze. And when that split second passed, I dragged her from the window. She was shaking. Fused with terror, so I hugged her tight.

'Don't touch me!' she cried. 'Take your meat hooks off!'

I was stunned. Maria hated me. Wanted no one near her. I felt sick. And a tear established in my eye.

I exhaled, exhausted. Then shouted to John. 'Check the rest of the house! Lock the doors. Bolt the windows.'

I turned to Maria. Her stare was *transfixed*. The intimidating figure of Alfred had disappeared, melted into nothing.

Subsequently, she sobbed. And it was only after her tears faded did she allow me to comfort her.

'Stephen. It came. Whatever it was, it came. Going to kill me. If it entered.'

'What! What came. I must know?'

Maria backed away, eyes dazed. 'Alfred!' She whispered as the name hung on the landing. 'His name… Alfred.' The 'name' suspended in the darkness like foul hanging meat.

'House secure!' yelled John. 'Stuck, Rex in the garden.'

'Thanks,' I replied. 'Hey! Find evidence of an intruder?'

'No! Nothing untoward. Everywhere's quiet.'

'Okay. Head home. I'll deal with it now.'

'No problem.' Then John exited.

Maria glanced. Our eyes met. And when they met, I stifled a gasp and flung a hand to my raw mouth, for I could not bear Maria's suffering. Next, sheer dread erupted. 'A… Al… Alfred's here! Wants us dead!' Then she declared, 'SOMETHINGS IN THIS GODDAMN *HOUSEEEEEEEEEEEEEE*!!!'

It was then I knew! That experiments conducted with the Diode machine to contact the dead had set free an electronic phenomenon. Evil. Paranormal. Gaining momentum. A momentum of its own nature which could not be controlled. In hindsight, I'd been a reckless clown for unleashing this terror.

Could I rationally explain the manifestation of Alfred, who died years ago? And appeared in full view of my wife? I'm afraid not! I was perplexed. My motives in ruins

After a kiss and a hug, we descended the stairs and entered the kitchen.

I telephoned the doctor. As I wanted, Maria checked. After a tense altercation, he agreed to the request.

Countless cigarettes later, the doctor arrived. He attended to Maria, performing a brief examination.

I dreaded what could happen. Could she be 'sectioned?' And require a stay in the hospital.

I feared I had sent her 'nuts' with the paranormal events occurring in the house. Misfortune lurked. Stalking! And it seemed ready to strike a fatal blow.

I repaired the door while the doctor conversed medical terms with Maria.

Twenty minutes passed—I waited impatiently. And the doctor arrived in the hallway for a discussion. 'Mr Reid. Given your wife thirty milligrams: Diazepam. In addition. Ten milligrams of Stelazine. An anti-psychotic. Has sedative tendencies. She's resting on the sofa. Should be calm. Probably sleep undisturbed through the rest of the night.'

'Will she recover?' I asked. 'Because, you mentioned anti-psychotics. Gets the alarm bells ringing.'

'My opinion. Your wife's suffering from acute stress. However, let's hit the point. Directly. For what it's worth? Now is she. Or you, sir. Partaking in drugs?'

'What's that supposed to mean?' I replied furiously. 'How ridiculous! We don't even smoke grass. And why, may I ask, are you fixated on street drugs?'

'Alright! Alright!' said the doctor. 'Didn't mean to imply anything untoward. Just wanted info. It supports diagnosis. Okay.'

The doctor paced a few steps. 'Think that, Mrs Reid,' he stated sternly. 'Should visit the surgery—next week. I may refer her to a psychiatrist. For assessment… Now forgive the last question—as your wife would not comment. But what triggered the hysteria?'

I went numb. Tingling sensations pinched. And I thought it best to hide the truth. Thus, I explained that a 'car killed her cat.' And this affected her.

The doctor flashed a wink—bid goodnight and exited the house, hastening to his car.

I shut the cracked door and backed against the rough board nailed upon it

I contemplated and prayed Maria hadn't relayed details about events in the house. It might have tempted the doctor to stick her in a mental institution. Also, God knows why he focused on drugs. That was unsettling, for I'd done various illegal substances. And now, when I reflect back, I regret ever indulging in those reckless antics.

The evening passed with no more disturbances. So, I checked on Maria lying on the couch, sleeping peacefully.

I placed a floral blanket over her. Then, gently positioned a duck feather pillow under the head and quickly removed tufts of carpet and broken ornaments that lay on the floor—caused by Rex during the ghostly episode.

Next, I removed a bottle of Napoleon brandy from the shelf and gently closed the lounge door.

Rex sat in the kitchen, his new habitat for tonight. I stroked him. He settled, then curled into a ball on the floor.

Crows disturbed the trees, owls hunted prey, and three hours dissipated.

However, and to my disgust, I'd drunk half a bottle of brandy in the bedroom. The frenzied-fuelled trials over the days had taken their toll. I was full of self-doubt. I'll-worth. Regret and rage. The temper inside was ready to consume me. Drag us to its raging core. The drinking had triggered the anger. I knew I should stop drinking. But I couldn't. I just could not!

Then something tripped when I finished another glass. I thumped my brow. Punched the bed before drunkenness and recklessness goaded us.

The radio emitted 'memory-laden tunes.' Nevertheless, I could not relax. Or remain composed. I arose from the bed and wandered through the doorway. The bedroom light illuminated my silhouette as a broken, bitter man, still clinging to crazy ideas, still carrying the half-empty bottle of brandy for support.

I went to the landing window where Maria encountered the ghost. I gazed hard. It seemed dark and quiet outside, with only the silver shine of moonlight polishing the star-filled sky.

Something, though, did not feel right. I pressed my face against the window in despair. Then suddenly, *I* felt an icy draft brush against us. I gnashed teeth. I gnashed them until a couple chipped! For I knew this presence must be *back! Back* in the house.

'Bastard!' I yelled with fury. 'You're still here. Used to getting want you want. Well, not this time. Gotta get through me!'

Infuriated and without inhibitions, I darted downstairs, flicked the switch for the power—snatched the keys, rushed upstairs, and unlocked the workshop.

I entered and turned on the lights, including the infamous Diode machine, before chewing my lip with anticipation.

The machine incensed us. I felt like a depraved mercenary, and I wanted blood! Wanted to kill everything—anything in the room.

'Here I am! Right at ya!' I yelled. 'Speak! I demand a response. Mellissa. Understand?' I leaned on the desk. 'Wish to utter something. You piece of shit?' No reply. I enraged. Went insane! Then words exploded like guns. 'Mellissa! Answer me! NOW!!!'

'A ghost in the machine,' she hissed, robotic-like. 'A ghost on your phone!' I dropped the brandy bottle. 'Who scared Maria?' A delay shadowed with interference.

'Alfred visited *your* house!'

I rounded the room—and confronted the Diode machine. 'You say... Alfred. It ain't the Alfred I knew. It's someone. Or something. Mimicking him. An obscene bastard. Spy's on Maria in the shower.' My emotions pounded. I revolved. Eyes pointed. Bullish stare, gunning for a response.

'Believe Stephen!' cried Mellissa. 'We live in the house. Walk in the mirror of desires. Dance with the ghosts of eternity.'

A male voice interjected. 'ALFRED HERE! Yer old mucker! I live.' An unearthly laugh followed. 'I ain't dead!'

Suddenly, an idea erupted. The old man 'promised' that he would answer a specific question when he died, confirming his identity had survived and dwelled in the Spirit World.

I tore into the bedroom and removed personal documents from a filing case. There! I found an envelope containing a scrap of paper from years ago. I opened it and read the phrase. *Time is the Essence. For the rest of my Duties.* This vague unimportant slogan was evidential and, if repeated, would prove without a doubt that Alfred had survived death: mentally intact. Instantly, I clutched the brown-stained paper and hurried to the workshop.

'If you're Alfred,' I shot, incensed. 'Declare the phrase? You stated. When alive. That proves your personality! Spirit! Has remained intact. Has survived physical death.'

Only 'whispering voices' and eerie radio interference transpired. Finally, I slammed a fist beside the Diode machine. 'Answer!' I demanded. ANSWER! You goddamn son of a bitch!'

Mellissa rasped, 'We can shout! From the "City of the Dead."'

'Spare the meaningless interrogation,' I raged. 'Alfred! Confirm identity. Prove it's you?'

'Dreams enter the soul. For a life is a thousand poems.'

I thumped my brow in criticism. 'Wrong! I have exactly what's written. From the original guy. You're sick! Twisted! Using electronics as an Ouija Board.'

'Two men you hated. Lay dead,' seared the Alfred imposter. 'For murder lurks as does vengeance! You wanted revenge. Wanted the scoundrels dead. And I… I did the bidding! Give homage. Stephen. Throw off the shackles of God! Ha. Ha. Ha!'

'What in heaven's name do you mean?' No response emerged. I countered with disgust. 'I do not believe the lies. The fakery. The impersonations. Everything's finished! Over! Whoever you are—I denounce your reality! You're nothing but myths. Only torment with lies.'

I grabbed the brandy bottle from the floor and screamed: 'I WANT THESE WRETCHED EXPERIMENTS TO *ENDDDDDDDDDDDDDD*!!!'

Mellissa rasped. 'You cannot deny our existence,' she asserted with rabidness. 'You're a fool! An ignorant man. Who wallows in dreams? And pathetic nostalgia. Who do you think you're dealing with? The link's strong! Focusing! Potent. All-pervading. *I* will soon manifest in the human world. And destroy you. Understand. UNDERSTAND!'

I went mad. Lost all restraint. 'DAMN YOU! DAMN YOUUUU!!! MELLISSA.'

'Someone stalks the house,' the entity raged. 'Ready to finish… your beloved Maria.'

'I'll end these idle threats. Now! Destroy the Diode machine. Smash it. Into a thousand pieces. Then consign you to the hellish realms! Where you belong!'

Suddenly, with that sentence, a diabolical change occurred. A loud growl. Unhuman. It resembled packs of crazed wolves tearing one another apart. Shaking intensified. The room vibrated. I glanced at the four corners and saw shadows darting upon the ceiling.

Something pounded on the roof. All the electronic devices flickered On and Off. And the lights followed. Then! As I tried to fight the disturbances. A horrific. Awful 'demonic groan' bellowed and howled, *'BOW BEFORE THE SPIRITS OF THE DEAD. IN THE ELECTRONIC REALM. WHERE GHOSTS LIVE. AND FERAL GODS RULEEEEEEEEE!!!'*

I wailed and threw the brandy bottle against the wall. It smashed into pieces, sending fragments of glass everywhere.

Next, I grabbed the Diode machine, but before moving it, a massive burst of electricity entered my body. Muscles went into spasms. Convulsions hit us. My arms ached. Yet, somehow, I managed with all strength to pull the mighty Diode machine from the desk and onto the ground, where it crashed apart.

Immediately, I stumbled and felt dazed.

Abruptly, the Fax Machine fashioned beeping noises, and a piece of paper emitted from the tray. I struggled up and pawed the sheet to my face.

My eyes packed with shock as I saw the blurred face of a woman on the sheet. Accompanied with the phrase, *You will perish! Reid. From the diabolic ghosts. Who dwells, in the electronic realm!*

Then, the tape machine reels spun anticlockwise and the entire workshop filled with scratching sounds.

Unexpectedly, all the lights failed, and an invisible force slammed me to the ground.

First, the door to the workshop creaked—preparing to seal us in. But splinters of glass wedged underneath the groove, preventing its closure.

Finally, static-like sparks sliced my face. I tried to fend off the assault. Next, something sprang onto my spine. It felt like an animal. I yelled. Then gazed behind for a moment before my head spun back. Suddenly frantic fear enveloped me when I witnessed a blue mist coalesce into a shape—ahead.

It illuminated parts of the darkened workshop. Unbelieving of its existence, I indeed felt it must be the alcohol. However, it was real.

In a blinding shooting flash, an apparition of a *cat* appeared. Tiger had revealed himself. Fully materialised. I rubbed a hand to my mouth, gasping with disbelief.

With all my strength, I scrambled from the floor and found a torch on the desk. A switch flicked. And I focused its beam on the crouched cat. Immediately, it released a dreadful shriek. Then its eyes packed with menace. Lastly, its fur exploded with fire— before the thing turned creamy white. It jumped and lashed out with decomposing paws—its slash marks drawing blood from my arms.

I cried in agony and bit my tongue to kill the pain. I went for the creature with bloodied hands—grappling, trying to trap it. The curtains in the workshop yanked from the windows while several tools blasted past. I shouted—then abruptly, the cat apparition vanished.

Somehow, I shoved an arm on the stirring door and regained balance. Before, a screwdriver darted through the air and struck the frame, missing us by inches.

I exited the scene, descended the stairs, and hurried to the fuse box under the stairway. I knew I had to censor the power and disrupt electricity in the workshop. Thus, I flicked the Off button. Bang! It did the trick. The main fuse short-circuited.

I heard objects smash against the house's foundations. And the workshop's floorboards rattle as if alive with poltergeists. These events continued for ages until an uneasy silence ended the disturbance.

I sighed. Exhaled wearily and slid down the wall. I sat on the carpet and remained there in deep, regretful thought for a long time.

My head sank into my quaking hands, and I sobbed in despair. Sobbing until I surrendered to a turbulent, exhausting sleep.

Chapter Eleven

Four days passed. Arguments exchanged. Explanations studied. And everything detailed to Gordon about the inexplicable events involving Maria and me. He understood our concerns and the unimaginable hell transpiring.

Therefore, Gordon contacted an expert with knowledge in this field of scientific phenomena. The scientist would inspect the house and conduct a thorough investigation to evaluate the incidents taking place.

The parapsychologist's official title was Dr Andreas Neilson, a lecturer at The Institute of Paranormal Research. London.

His parents were half-German—half-English, mixing his bloodline. He bore the stature of a tall, well-built man peppered with scars from latter middle age. A trimmed beard shadowed part of the doctor's face, and his brown hair swept neatly from the brow.

Gordon accompanied Dr Neilson along the path and to the front door.

The late afternoon sunshine reflected upon the scientist's spectacles. Thus, he removed them and unbuttoned his chequered tweed jacket.

Dr Neilson's skill in paranormal science always gave him uplifting confidence before any case.

He *gazed* at the red brick house and trod the driveway

interestedly. A shoulder bag hung on his shoulder, containing electronic devices he used in his ghostly work. Then Dr Neilson knocked on the house door.

I sat anxiously with Maria in the living room, dreading this man's arrival. Feelings tense—the feelings gurgling and leaking within the chest, rendering me speechless. Next, apprehension gnawed at the gut. Gradually, I arose and consoled Maria. 'That'll be Gordon. With Dr Neilson. I'll see to the door. Try an act rationally.' Maria agreed with a tense nod, and I exited.

A 'brief greeting' transpired, and I invited both into the house. Maria heard conversations. Gordon first, then me, and to finish the scientist. She took a deep breath and tried to remain calm—a tremendous achievement—because of the disturbances.

Abruptly, the silhouette of a man outlined in the doorway. It grew. And Dr Andreas Neilson entered. He fixed his square spectacles onto the eyes, and to Maria, he resembled the actor Orson Welles.

'Dr Neilson! Thanks for coming,' she said unreservedly.

The guest smiled. Winked and removed a black bag from his shoulder. He gave the nod. Then introduced himself. 'Pleasure's all mine, Mrs Reid. By the way. I'm on first-name terms in any investigation. So, call me Andreas. Won't take offence.'

'Okay! Like a drink Dr Neilson?... Sorry I meant Andreas?' Dr Neilson rubbed his hands confidently. 'Could sure use whisky? Neat. Helps concentration.' He released a slight chuckle.

Maria agreed. 'Stephen. Be a love,' she began. 'Take a seat with Gordon. Don't worry. I'll sort the beverages.'

'No problem. Honey.'

Elsewhere, Dr Neilson asked Gordon to pass various technical papers. And he read intensely. Afterwards, his eyes met mine sternly. 'Before drinks, Mr Reid. Want to inspect the room. In the house. Where experiments took place. Your electronic experiments, to be exact.'

'By all means. Anyway. The name's Stephen. We're all on first-name terms now.' We bantered for a while when Maria entered and placed drinks on the coffee table. Next, she explained she had to pop next door and see Carol. 'Fine, Maria,' I said. 'Catch up on all the gossip.'

'Sure will.'

The front door closed, and I got up—hastening to the hallway, beckoning at Dr Neilson. He acknowledged. Gripped his black bag and followed. I progressed the winding staircase and glanced behind. Dr Neilson trailed in measured succession; I think his weight affected him as heavy breaths emitted from taxed lungs. Nevertheless, we continued onward until finally reaching the workshop.

'Trouble's been brewing for weeks,' I said. 'But hit a crescendo! Went Mad! A few days ago. All started when Tiger. Our cat freaked out in the workshop. For no rational—'

'—Rational!' finished Dr Neilson. 'Wait, Stephen. *Cats* are sensitive to anything. Be it spiritual or paranormal. Wouldn't go berserk. Without provocation.'

'Interesting observation. Anyhow. Cat's dead. Run—'

'—Please, Stephen, already know,' finished Dr Neilson again. 'There's no time for sob stories. We gotta focus! On the job at hand…!'

I got irritated. The doctor's abrupt responses were curt. Yet, I cast them aside. 'If I can mention,' I began. 'A couple of nights ago. Everything kicked off. Total mayhem. My wife witnessed a man. Ghost! At the landing window… unsurprisingly! For I sensed something alien. In the workshop. A day earlier. Watching. Invisible to the eye. And it attacked us.'

'Understand the concern, Stephen. Read the "report." From Gordon. Documenting the Diode machine and spirit voices. Communicating. Tormenting. Throwing things.'

I exhaled wearily. Unfastened the lock and flung the workshop door sideward, sending it crashing against the wall.

Dr Neilson entered. And observed different instruments and

equipment scattered. However, the one item that gripped attention was the infamous, reddish-brown, metal-encased Diode machine. It could've come straight from a science fiction movie.

It rested on the floor. Still in the exact position. The very place where I left it.

Dr Neilson put his black bag on a workshop shelf. Unzipped it and removed an electronic device. Then, after completing this chore—pushed a button. Instantly, his electronic instrument powered On. And went live. Functioning perfectly. Circumspect bleeps and crackling noises followed, and the doctor made adjustments while observing the broken Diode machine.

He pointed a stern stare. 'So! This is the troublesome machine. Solely constructed! To enable two-way conversation with the Spirit World.'

'Spot on!'

'Understand what I'm about to say, Stephen! No one! Ever achieved this type of spirit communication. Only Patrick O Brennen and Liam T Nelson were successful.... Now,' added Dr Neilson. 'I've listened to the tapes. Gordon gave. I experimented with the acoustics and must admit. The voice of *Mellissa*. And this *Alfred personality* is the most impressive example of recorded speech I have heard—in decades of tireless research.'

I felt elated. Thrilled after Dr Neilson's comments. My results from the Diode machine had 'the stamp of approval' from a scientist. Nevertheless, I could not let this compliment distract attention from the nightmare episode. I wanted everything paranormal gone—exorcised from the house, religiously.

Dr Neilson, with difficulty, turned the Diode machine on its side and used the electronic device to scan the casing.

Suddenly, the doctor's device erupted before I could catch my breath.

'Crikey! What's that! Ticking like a bomb?'

'In scientific terms. A power-driven eye and ear. If there's something here! This instrument will nail it! Detect any energy surge… Right!' he added. 'Fasten the door. Wait outside. Until further instruction.'

'Surely not a wise option? You know the situation?'

'Do as requested! Without delay!'

I reluctantly acknowledged, exited, and dragged the door shut. Dr Neilson checked the workshop, rotating his head to the side.

Next, he listened for anything audible. Nothing! Then he noticed the upturned reel-to-reel tape recorder and splinters of glass from the brandy bottle. In conclusion, he observed the Diode machine for a moment.

Suddenly, his electronic instrument ignited, and the readings flashed red. Dr Neilson peered at the four corners of the room before itchy sensations rubbed his neck.

I rapped on the door. Abruptly the doctor berated, 'Don't disturb! I'm engaged in procedures.'

Dr Neilson's attention re-focused. He grabbed the recorder and tried removing the reel of magnetic tape. He only touched the stuff for a second when a static charge raced through his arm.

The doctor's electronic instrument glinted! Burned! And he dropped it. The doctor's eyes fixated, and he witnessed the gadget jerk from side to side on the floor. Then, while preparing to document the event, it darted like a thunderbolt, rearwards, smashing against the skirting board.

The Diode machine powered On. Surreal sounds exploded with menace, and a thick electrical humming followed. The air permeated with charred wires before the phrase *Mellissa Is Here!* United into a chorus.

As no electricity entered the machine, Dr Neilson noted— contemplated and made a judgement about this mysterious phenomenon.

My curiosity intensified. This stranger had no right mulling in the workshop. I couldn't hold back. I wanted in! Thus, I lost patience. Banged ajar the door and yelled, 'Here! Listen. I wanna know about the wretched ghosts! It's my house! Not a goddamn

Edwardian seance!' Dr Neilson's arm twitched. Shook and motioned beyond control. Then suddenly, his right hand balled, reopened and snatched my green shirt, slamming us to the floor. 'What the hell! What're you doing?' I snapped. 'Release us!'

'CAN'T!' strained Dr Neilson. 'Lost control. The unexplained is unveiled! IT'S REAL! Something's attacking!'

'Cut the joke! Ain't funny!' I raged. 'See the—' Any humorous notions dissipated when a mighty thud struck the doctor.

'SHITTT! YOU THINK THIS A JOKE?' cried Dr Neilson, eyes bloodshot, mouth twitching. 'I'M NOT PLAYING AROUND! BREAK THE LINK. IT'S USING US FOR MALEVOLENT DEEDS.'

I thought Dr Neilson had lost his wits. However, this notion vanished when an invisible fist struck my jaw, accompanied by a loud smack.

Next, poltergeist activity arose, and the Diode machine rocked and bounced as if springs gravitated underneath.

'Gordon!' I yelled. 'Shift your arse. Get here! There's trouble! Big Trouble!'

A shout! The stairs pounded, and my mate entered. He freed us from the doctor, then ducked as a spinning hammer flew past.

'Out! Leave!' demanded Dr Neilson. 'Show's finished!' He lifted his damaged electronic device and exited.

Gordon and I trailed, escaping from whatever loitered in the workshop. I slammed the door. And a massive object sealed onto it.

'There shouldn't be activity?' challenged Dr Neilson. 'You stated. Power's off!'

'Supposed to be.' I squinted at Gordon. 'Check the electrics! The fuse box. Then wait for Maria. She'll be home anytime soon.'

'Okay.' Quickly, he descended the staircase.

The doctor and I remained. He paced, soldier-like, pondering.

I straightened up. 'Did anything,' I said inquisitively. 'Manifest?'

Dr Neilson halted. 'Yes! Atmospheric phenomenon. It had life!' He released a nervous chuckle to break the tension. 'I've experienced similar phenomena before. But never with that impact. Especially in daytime. Normally,' he added, 'it's dead of night. When this type of psychokinesis occurs.' Dr Neilson gazed at his device, digesting the readings—checking damage inflicted from the unseen force, 'Stephen,' he said. 'Make your way to the living room. I'll join you. Soon.'

I agreed with a wink. Departed and left the doctor to his thoughts and problems.

Thirty minutes later, Maria and Gordon waited in the lounge sipping drinks, conversing earnestly—while I had a hint of brain fog.

Dr Neilson entered. He didn't say a thing. Next, he gulped the rest of his whisky.

I felt uneasy. So acted hospitably. 'For what it's worth. Wanna another pick-me-up?'

'No! Had enough,' he uttered. Then he exhaled and hastened to the centre of the room. 'Everybody. A lecture's due—to be precise, a serious talk! Fun and games are over. We're on a risky journey. Our safety rests—on action taken this day.'

We all placed our glasses on the coffee table and went mute, like dumb students, because we did not know what to expect.

'Where's your dog?'

'Rex! In the care of my sister,' answered Maria, downcast. 'Thought it best. Y'know? Keep him from harm's way.'

The doctor's features creased, and his intimidating presence strengthened. 'The situation with these disturbances. Experienced first-hand. And the tapes that Gordon gave, with spirit voices captured by Stephen. Has led me to this conclusion.'

'What's that?' I asked.

'Electronic Voice Phenomenon and Spiricom. The detailed construction. Of a machine to contact the dead from another dimension is a notorious science. Dismissed by psychics, mediums, and the clergy, as dabbling with an electronic occult… Yet, it's a proven method. Or a way of penetrating the sphere where departed souls of people who once lived on this Earth reside.' Dr Neilson's aura rose with authority, and he treaded methodically.

Gordon sneered, amused by this lecture. The doctor threw a stare of rage. 'Something funny. Think you're better practised than I? More informed to pass judgment?'
My friend lost his cynical attitude. And went receptive.

'There are experimenters around the world,' continued Dr Neilson. 'Who've used various instruments in electronic spirit communication? With many receiving amazing results. An institute in Switzerland… *IBNT* for short. Have invested heavily in a new audio-visual device called, Videocom.'

Interested, I uttered, 'What… What's Videocom?'

'A way. With video cameras—and televisions tuned to a channel. Not receiving broadcast signals. To collect pictures and images from the "other side." Named the Astral Timestream. The Astral Timestream is a spirit technician's station. Furthermore, due to this incredible discovery, qualified pseudoscientists have initiated exchanges. Recorded deceased people on videotape. Many prominent historical figures have appeared, including Jules Verne, Charles Dickens, plus others too numerous to mention.'

The doctor paused and corrected himself. 'One moment! I must not forget a vital individual. Frederick Jurgheson. The architect of this unexplained phenomenon.' The doctor removed several pictures from his bag and handed them for inspection.

The pictures were truly unique, though certain things puzzled me. For example, if these prominent people died in the early 1900s and were now in contact, why were their clothes in the spirit pictures encompassing typical 1980s suits, including a thin black leather tie?

Gordon made this 'point' to Dr Neilson—but the doctor countered with some answer, explaining they did this to be acceptable. More in tune with the present decade.

I must admit I found Dr Neilson's answers awkward and evasive of facts—nevertheless, I kept the prejudices to myself.

Maria studied one image. Then asked a hesitant question. 'So… I've focused on the pictures… and heard what you've said. But what's this got to do with the mysterious circumstances? And events of destruction arising in Stephen's workshop?'

'I'll explain, Maria,' replied Dr Neilson. 'You can say that it takes all sorts to create a world. There are comedians, pranksters, and the most treacherous of all—entities who want to create disorder in one's mind. A psychological attack. This applies to the other side, or spirit world, as it's generally referred to in psychic circles. To be specific, it goes like this.'

The doctor's voice increased. His eyes went solemn. And he acted like a resilient politician. 'There are seven heavens in the world beyond. Transitions,' he began. 'Or a state of mind where certain individuals go. When they die, most people awake and find themselves in the second heaven. It's a resting place where people adjust and learn before they progress to the next stage of the heavenly plane. These people have contacted researchers and given wise and informative advice on the sphere they now inhabit.'

He pondered for reflection, then recommenced. 'Now, that does not concern us, in this instance.'

'Why's that?' I asked.

'Because Stephen. We're dealing with the first heaven, or lower astral plane, as it is sometimes called? It is a kind of living hell place of purgatory and regret. Here you'll find criminals. Sex perverts. Confused or materially obsessed individuals—desperate to gain access to their physical things. But can't anymore as their precious commodities are beyond reach. If I can be specific, the more evil a person is, the more they'll attract similar entities. Ones who fester and multiply in a hellish-type dimension. This part of the astral plane is closest to earth. And thus, easier to message… I've heard recordings of the robotic voices. And my verdict is!

Some form of contact has been established. Stephen's the beacon—and these malevolent entities have latched onto him.'

'What! I can't be sure of the implications,' I replied, using my own spin. 'It specifically states in books. These electronic audio-visual ghosts, or entities. Only emerge from a spirit transmission station. Positioned on the other side. And cannot enter from an unproven source.'

'Listen carefully,' stated Dr Neilson, eyes stern. 'If someone's inexperienced in the procedure of electronic voice phenomenon. And conducts experiments without care. They'll invite a destructive force. That lurks in the lower astral realms. And *IT* will use all its devious ploys to suck the investigator into a web of sinister discussions. Thus, it'll gain power from the emotions of fear, rage, and deceit. So markedly, and eventually, it will break free from its morbid existence and attack the experimenter for its own perverse gratification. I dealt with a case in France where a man went insane. By hearing non-human voices. Not due to the tapes he made but from inside his head. The symptoms resembled "paranoid schizophrenia." Now explain, Stephen, what did you feel when conversing with the Alfred personality? On the comments he articulated?'

I thought, then answered. 'It wasn't him... well, the Alfred I once knew.'

Dr Neilson's next question intensified. 'Now! This is very important. What did you feel? Sense about Mellissa's personality? Remember. That's the entity or ghost! Which first, and most importantly, initiated the two-way conversation with your Diode machine?'

'Without a shadow of a doubt. Sinister!'

'Then the feelings are justified, Stephen. Evil spirits cannot deceive the human instinct.'

I glanced at Maria, then at Dr Neilson. 'Sir. I'm concerned—the image of the Alfred personality, my wife, witnessed. Pressed against the landing window. What the hell was it?'

'By opinion. And on what Maria described—' Dr Neilson paused, menace built within the room before he unleashed a dreaded, dramatic reply. 'An earthbound demon! That's escaped. Found a way to manifest in our world. Aided by the Diode machine.' The doctor's answer was shocking. Fear crossed Maria's eyes. Her skin snowed white, and tears trickled upon her cheeks.

The comments by Dr Neilson unnerved us all—terrifying with their clarity. I found it tough to remain rational after what this paranormal scientist stated. The whole thing seemed like a horror movie. Then I remembered a passage from an Electronic Voice Phenomenon journal and how the writer gave the reader a blunt warning.

The Electronic Voice Phenomenon is a recognized science—however, there is a risk with this exercise. I strongly advise and cannot accept responsibility if people undertake this research before reading the facts essential to this process. Therefore, I no longer engage in E.V.P. I've obtained enough proof and wish to leave it.

I suppose a person's own choice and viewpoint make us question what becomes of us after we die. Humanity has been searching throughout the ages to find the answers to this question. Of course, there are different answers to this through the many religions. But the prospect of receiving Spirit messages through electronic means is a fantastic development. How far will it progress? Who knows?

Thus, after recalling lines from the journal and listening to Dr Neilson's lecture, I could not disregard the facts—unveiled! Specified and explained with eloquence.

All previous disbeliefs about ghosts and life after death had vanished. I knew any sane explanation to dismiss the paranormal issues of 'Electronic Voice Phenomenon', and 'Spiricom' were no longer valid. The disturbing events of the last few weeks had proved my undoing.

There is definitely some kind of cosmic sphere where the souls of the dead and other non-human creatures inhabit. It could be the third sphere—some time travel dimension. Or perhaps, Inner Space.

Dr Neilson's scientific sermon had ended the hoax theory! It wasn't a radio nut or prankster playing tricks. So, unfortunately, demons and ghosts do exist! I just wondered what the guy might say next.

Dr Neilson's brow furrowed—eyes pointed stern. 'Now, friends! It's up to us! To banish this force! Send it back to where it came. Gordon, search the van outside. Bring video cameras. And the main TV monitors in the house. Hopefully, we'll be able to mount the cameras along the staircase. And I'll try and fathom, deliberate, on what other equipment's required.'

Gordon toyed! Unsure. Sceptical. He had severe doubts about what stirred in Dr Neilson's head. Therefore, either the doctor was a renowned expert. Or possessed the mind of a mad man.

'A pointed excuse!' began Gordon. 'You're getting ahead. I mean. Who do you think you are? An Electronic Exorcist!'

My friend's comment angered Dr Neilson, and he countered with disapproval. 'Don't make stupid comments! This stuff is something you don't screw around with!' He paused and reflected before continuing. 'The true consequences of what we're dealing with are extreme! Dangerous! Deadly. There's no time for levity,' he exclaimed, phrase brutal.

I intervened. 'C'mon! Gordon. Knock it off!'

After prostrations, my friend exited and went to Dr Neilson's van.

I motioned to Maria. 'Suggest honey. You've been through enough! Last few days. Why don't you stay with Janice? Your sister. Only for a day or so? Until we extinguish this ghostly episode.'

'No!'

'Okay. How about John and Carol? The neighbours. They'd love the company.'

'Stephen! Yer don't listen. No! I won't. This is my house. My home! And I'm not going to allow it—be torn apart by you lot,' she added stubbornly. 'Anyhow. I've seen Alfred. That horrible thing once. So! Wanna give payback. He ain't gonna terrorise again. I remain here! Stephen.' She cradled my hand. Then her eyes fastened onto mine, and at that moment, our love intensified, as did our hearts, beating as one.

'Maria,' I exhaled, 'I'm worried. On what'll happen.'

Dr Neilson interjected. 'Stephen. A penny for your thoughts. Your wife has the patience of a saint—courage of a soldier. And got guts. Especially after recent events. Mrs Reid. I salute you.' A smile crossed his face.

'That's settled then!' I said. 'A wife is a wife. She wants to stay! And stay, she will.'

Dr Neilson's expression strained. He mumbled! Uttered a German phrase and glimpsed at his gold-strapped watch. 'We better go. And do work, Stephen. Please! Excuse us, Maria. Things need attention.'

We both left the lounge, exited the house, and hurried to Gordon, assisting him with the electronic equipment in the van.

Afterwards, the miniature blue *China Doll* resting on the ornate fireplace caught Maria's vision. It originated from Alfred. And was one of only a few ornaments that survived the fracas with Rex and Tiger. She wondered with weary intuitions if it, her, or anybody, would survive the forthcoming night unscathed.

Chapter Twelve

The clock in the hallway displayed nine o'clock p.m. Thus, the late evening crept upon us like soundless owls.

Gordon had stuck a few video cameras on the wall round the staircases.

One bulky camera, fixed with sturdy brackets—was situated atop the staircase, and another—opposite the workshop.

Two televisions, acting as monitors, were sited downstairs in the hallway, amongst various electronic dials and devices. And an assortment of other gadgets rested on a makeshift table that Dr Andreas Neilson constructed.

A reel-to-reel tape recorder nestled beside a couple of radios— plus an electronic temperature graph reader bleeped. So this completed the assortment of audio-visual equipment.

Everything was readied to the doctor's requirements. Next, Gordon twisted a screwdriver and tweaked one video camera secured near the staircase.

My friend called Dr Neilson, whose *eyes* busied—anxiously checking the electronic gadgets he owned. Another Diode machine created by a colleague at the university where he lectured—sited in the middle of the table.

The doctor explained he'd never obtained the results I'd achieved with my Diode machine. Consequently, Dr Neilson wanted to replicate the same results with his equipment for morbid gratification. And direct a two-way conversation with the entity, ghost, creating havoc in the house.

Abruptly, Gordon's voice filtered within a speaker. 'Corrected networks. You getting pictures on the TVs?'

Dr Neilson sweated with anticipation. He fixed position, studied a monitor, and adjusted one volume dial. The buttons for Brightness and Contrast rotated clockwise, and the doctor saw Gordon on camera—meticulously fitted. Then, with an enthusiastic thrill, he voiced, 'Yes! Exquisitely done! Not as stupid as you act. Despite recent sarcasm!' He then asked Maria and me to join him. 'Come. Leave the kitchen. Things await.'

I replaced the coffee cup and stepped from the dish-laden pantry with Maria.

I went to Dr Neilson and peered at the television monitors. I must admit I *felt* amazed, which I knew was absurd, for Dr Neilson and Gordon had professionally put together the whole shebang.

'Everything ready?' I asked inquisitively. 'Can see. By the way the video cameras are secured. Directed to a position. Prepared for recordings?'

Maria stood still—holding back. I think the video cameras and the gadgetry instilled unease. Perchance, she sensed! Dreaded something paranormal erupting any moment.

I smiled to ease the pressure and beckoned her nearer.

Dr Neilson gyrated his backside with discomfort. I'm sure he suffered from haemorrhoids. But did not dare ask.

Then the atmosphere electrified when he drilled a marked stare. 'Stephen! We're prepared for procedures to go ahead—with all the evil spirits and ghosts in the vicinity. Watching! Listening! We must hold our nerve. Steady wits.... We are going to undertake a hell of a journey. There'll be no time for jokes. And this isn't a game. We are in this for the long haul. So! Act precisely! In any way, I deem fit.'

'Okay. Name what's on the agenda. What we're supposed to do?' I replied. 'Remember! Never engaged with someone—with your scientific expertise... My knowledge of the electronic voice phenomenon stems from books and journals.'

The doctor stole a glance at the screens. 'When Gordon's done—aligning the final camera. Reconnect power to the workshop.'

'Is that wise?'

'Just do it! I know what to expect.'

Gordon descended the staircase, past Maria, before kneeling by the side of Dr Neilson. He studied the television pictures and felt proud of his achievement.

All the electronic stuff was functioning. 'Not a bad job. If I don't say. No idea know what you're expecting?' reiterated Gordon. 'But whatever... be it human or paranormal? The video cameras will catch it. Perhaps Harry Houdini, or King Henry The VIII, might surprise us with an appearance.' He guffawed loudly.

'Fool!' remarked Dr Neilson with displeasure. 'This is not trickery! Or a reality show. Idiot.'

The turn of the phrase infuriated Gordon after the hard work he'd completed. 'Great! Thanks a bunch. I take offence easy—if it weren't for me! Pal. You'd never have known about Stephen's experiments. Ungrateful, German tosser!'

Dr Neilson's face crossed with rage. He rose and readied a right hook.

Quickly I intervened. 'Christ! Mate. For *God's* sake! Cut it out! Stop fighting.' I glared with daggers. 'Listen! What is it with you? What's the damn problem, Gordon? C'mon. Man up! I mean it.' I flashed a stare. Subsequently, his arrogance faded.

'Alright! Stephen,' he retorted. 'Get the drift. Remember though. Ain't doing this to suffer insults. Worked my bollocks off tonight.'

I perceived a rivalry between Dr Neilson and Gordon. But did not know from where it came. Possibly they had a history—a story of conflicting opinions.

The atmosphere cooled. Dr Neilson huffed with indifference—and knocked switches on the silver-control board. Pictures spread apart from each camera. An awkward pause transpired, and he instructed Gordon to recheck the video machine connections—to measure signal interference.

Maria stepped up for a better view as my friend fiddled with the audio-visual apparatuses. He adjusted screws. Fixed capacitors to a circuit board. Tested audio needles. Fastened headphones. Enhanced the sensitivity of the microphones—and signified that operations were ready. 'Everything's set!' he stated strongly. 'Prepared for action. See no more problems.'

Dr Neilson pointed. 'Stephen. Relink electricity. Replace the fuse. Then flick the Main switch for the workshop. Everything has to be activated. We commence battle with the spirits! Now!'

I shivered and felt unsettled while emotions stirred and faintness lurked. Evil thoughts of what could happen made me sick. Yet, I agreed to the doctor's request with whatever misconceptions I had.

I paced to the fuse box, carefully avoiding wires and plugs. Waited a second and steered a steely glare at the doctor.

His gaze met mine. And at that moment, the gravity of the situation slammed upon us. 'Do as I demand,' he implored. 'Flick the damn switch.'

I nodded. Placed my left hand on the fuse box—then suddenly, a blue spark of light erupted from space, dazzling the dust in the air—carrying like a fleeing ghost. A sharp shock travelled within my arm. I panted. My body jolted backwards. 'SHIT!!! What the hell?'

Maria dashed forward. 'Stephen! Honey! You hurt?'

I exhaled a relieved sigh. 'Maria! Slightly shaken. But otherwise. Still in order.' I turned to Dr Neilson. 'Why'd you instruct us to do that? Y'know!' I explained. 'The instant power enters the workshop. Something supernatural occurs.'

'Mr Reid. Don't question motives. I'm aware of the malevolent force... Here.' I steadied my nerve. 'So! What's the strategy, doctor? Precisely. What'll we do in the meantime?'

'Wait. And be patient. I need to reflect.' Dr Neilson stood and went to a camera on the staircase.

****

A couple of hours passed, and everything remained quiet. Gordon relaxed in the lounge, talking clairvoyance stories with Maria—which seemed odd. However, I wanted a personal chat with Dr Andreas Neilson. I desired info from his past—on what inspired him? To engage in this ghostly scientific phenomenon.

I approached with questioning eyes. 'Excuse me. Hope it's not intrusive. But. Can you give us an insight!? Y'know. Your background in the paranormal?' I added. 'From the science angle. The personal experiences that drive you. Make you participate in electronic voice phenomenon and spiricom?'

Dr Neilson's face rose from a *Psychic Magazine*. He frowned before addressing us. 'Be it known, Stephen. Once I was at a conference with technical experts. Who challenged Konstantin Raudive on the spirit voices he captured? He presented evidential tapes. Recorded. Used in his research. We conducted numerous tests,' added Dr Neilson. 'Under strict laboratory conditions, to check for deception. The investigators of "German psychic research", GPR—desperately wanted him nailed! For fraud. But the scientist confounded all critics. And we had no alternative to accept as fact—the results Raudive achieved. That's what got us involved with this paranormal research. But it's not the only unusual subject that ensnared fascination. When but a lad. My mother. Who practised as a spiritualist medium—held seances— to contact the deceased? I watched strange events unfold. But at one sitting that I didn't attend—on my fourteenth birthday, to be exact. My mother went into a trance. And a spirit, or ghost, call it what you will entered her.'

'What did it say?' I asked, enthralled.

'Won't go into complete detail. However, the "spirit" claimed to be from a person. Involved with the expedition party. That Major Gregory Phillips took to the deserts of Egypt.'

'Wait a minute!' I commented. 'I read about Gregory Phillips. A British explorer who travelled to the Amazon jungle in the 1880s to find a city of unknown riches. Located in a pyramid—built by an alien race. That compressed their skulls into weird shapes. The book stated native tribal Indians killed him.'

At that moment, I remembered passages from that same book.

Major Gregory Phillips: Fact Or Fiction

Major Phillips enlisted in the British army in his youth and served in various countries. Phillips always had an interest in the paranormal and read numerous occultist magazines.

Shortly after the Crimean War in 1856, he read a report of a 1689 expedition that entered the Amazonian Rainforest—searching for an underground city—holding many amazing treasures. The advanced civilization was said to be highly intelligent and may have been descendants of the lost city of Atlantis.

This story fascinated him, and the mystique and secrecy appealed to his adventurous nature. So, in 1874, he made arrangements for an expedition into the South American jungle—to provide detailed proof to the outside world—of this mysterious civilization.

Nevertheless, Phillips and his party were poorly supplied when entering the Amazon basin. They headed north past Bogota and then east, making camp at the 'Pyramid of the Dead' spot. The Major made an average entry in his diary about eating and the troublesome bugs. However, this was his last message as neither he nor his party would ever be heard of again.

No undue concern transpired because he was not supposed to return until 1878.

In 1921, an expedition party from the USA led by Bernard Jacobs set off—searching for the Phillips mission. They got to the 'Pyramid of the Dead' camp and encountered local Indians, who gave a somewhat whimsical story that the Major had traversed further into the jungle. Jacobs seemed convinced that Major Phillips and his researchers had fallen prey to vicious Indians.

Twenty years later, Harrison Morrison, the famous Australian explorer, entered the Amazon to see what happened to Phillips. After two days, he encountered the Kalapolo Tribe about nine miles from the 'Pyramid of the Dead' camp. Morrison extracted a confession from the Kalapolo chief, who admitted they had speared the Major to death. They passed some remains to the party to provide proof of the story.

A few months later, Morrison managed to get the remains examined by a pathologist in Sydney. The pathologist compared them with the Major's medical details and found them not to be Phillips. Maybe the final conclusion to the story lies with the well-known medium, Mrs Stephanie Fontana. In 1931, some family relatives handed her a scarf worn by the Major. Using psychometry, she immediately had a trance vision of Phillips and the party savagely attacked and killed, then their bodies thrown into a swamp.

A book published by Phillips' daughter in 1962, called *Investigation Philips*, was a collection of her father's notes and journals. And is the last known book published about the Major.

A stage play was made on Phillips and staged in New York. The theatre producer had access to secret papers held by the Phillips family and even went to the spot where the Major disappeared.

I have always found the story about Phillips intriguing. Unfortunately, however, it is irrelevant to E.V.P.

Perhaps, though, someone has obtained an E.V.P. message after entering the Amazon jungle armed with a tape recorder—and then disappeared!

I remained in thought until Dr Neilson startled us with a tap on the cheek. 'Lost in space?'

'Sorry. Pray continue, doctor.'

'Okay,' he replied, assured. 'So! The story about the Major consumed me. Suppose that's what fastened interest. At such a young age—with the ludicrous idea of exploring possibilities. On what happened to the Major and the others.

"When mother died, I inherited a small fortune, and after studying maps and books on *Major Gregory Phillips,* I became obsessed. Intrigued about his expedition. Thus, I arranged my own in 1964 to examine how he died.

Nevertheless, our adventure was ill-planned and beset by problems when we entered Bolivia. What with the heat and disease, which eliminated half the expeditionary force? The rest of us encountered hostile Amazonian Indians further into the forest, past the "Pyramid of the Dead" encampment: the place described by the Major in his diary before he disappeared. The situation deteriorated and cost one man his life when the Indians stole equipment. My dear friend Professor Wolfgang Peterson tried to persuade our antagonists to return the items, but they speared him in the stomach during a heated row. I witnessed his pleading face and tried to save him! But arrows and sticks fired by these Indians beat us back. Then a rock smashed into his head—killing him. Finally, I witnessed his body dragged into the jungle, held aloft in triumph by the Indians. The remaining colleagues in the party screamed that all of us had to escape. If only to save our lives.

Consequently, we abandoned the whole nauseating adventure. This not only disappointed us, particularly the death of a friend— but also because I'd used most of the money from my inheritance that funded the expedition. The German Press ridiculed my antics, and I faced a lawsuit from the widow of Professor Wolfgang Peterson, which left us penniless. And further humiliation followed—as fellow academics and scientists briefed Universities. Making outlandish accusations. These people's despicable lies eventually drove me from Germany. And I went to the USA, before eventually settling in England.'" Dr Neilson sighed deeply, and his head bowed.

I understood his trauma and felt profound sympathy.

Gradually, the doctor regained dignity and hastened the narrative to a conclusion. 'Now, Stephen. That nightmare taught me one thing! Don't accept advice from any spirit. My ill-fated Phillips escapade proved that. Any information given from a "Medium" treat cynically. This equates to other means. Like electronic communication! Be objective, but be cautious. That's what I recommend—as I've witnessed many outbreaks of paranormal activity.'

I marvelled at what this big man relayed—he'd experienced intriguing events. We talked further—then Gordon entered and asked if anything else wanted scrutiny?

Hours passed listlessly as I rested in the living room. Then, between fleeting squints, I noticed the time. It was One o'clock a.m. 'Time's a strange tool,' I thought aloud. 'Travels in mysterious ways. Wonder if the dead are aware. Of its ticking presence—in the realm they inhabit.'

Gordon chatted with Dr Neilson in the hallway and adjusted screws, buttons and wires—fixed with a screwdriver and hammer.

Both observed automated readings and acoustic needles move back and forth on the control panel with awe.

'Interesting. Interesting,' murmured the doctor. He seized a pen and quickly noted the temperature on the thermometer

A click! I tensed. And realised I was still awake—sat in the lounge—light-headed. Maria had dozed off, and we snuggled tight on the sofa—left hands clasped. I briefly glimpsed sideward and witnessed lights shimmering and gleaming from the hallway.

Gordon poked Dr Neilson's arm. 'Going outside. I wanna drag! A cigarette. You mind?'

'Be quick! Something's stirring!'

Gordon agreed with a nod and exited. He strolled on the damp grass, smelt the night air and peered ahead.

Next, he removed a Camel cigarette packet, rolled the paper, and tapped one coffin stick out of the box. The flint sparked, and the cigarette flamed blue. Gordon smoked intensely; then dizziness ensued due to nicotine.

The wind increased as if a weathering storm waited on the horizon, and trees across the way moved apart in varied directions.

Nocturnal wildlife agitated, and a fox darted close as if disturbed by *something*. Then, it steadied and waited before skurrying into the thick undergrowth. Gordon coughed, whistled, and paced to Dr Neilson's van—watching a mass of circling moths.

I drifted in and out of sleep in the living room and found it tough to relax. However, Maria had no problem.

My eyes flickered, and I stretched, muscles aching. Maria snuggled on my shoulder, and I tried not to disturb her.

Abruptly, I felt uneasy! As if observed by *something monstrous*. I shivered. Then suddenly, I saw boots pounding on a grave. Next, a cemetery arose, with mist forming—packed with swirling phantoms exhibiting evil stares. I went shocked! Breaths were raw. Then the vision petered away like a sinister chapter from a horror novel.

****

Outside, Gordon finished the cigarette. Crushed the smoking butt with his shoe and headed to the house. Suddenly, his attention fixated on an older adult gliding along the windswept road. Also, a strange dark bird with an orange glow appeared and perched on the neighbour's fence.

Gordon puzzled. Features confused, first because of the bird, second because of the man dressed oddly in a black 'Nazi SS uniform'. Then finally, he chuckled. However, his flippancy was ill-judged, for the unfolding events would unleash terror.

The old man was Alfred's evil twin. The demonic entity who had confronted Maria.

Unexpectedly, a chill in the air seized Gordon's lungs. He released a gasp. Then the 'cry' of an unholy force hit a crescendo—a crescendo of malice.

Abruptly, the entity stopped. That was its cue. It cast a wicked, baleful stare and edged closer.

Maria awakened. She noticed tiny lights and heard Dr Neilson's electronic gadgets beeping and squeaking. The noise amplified the unease—shooting to every corner of the house. She expected! Sensed something unblessed waiting. Nevertheless, she dispelled the notion with a yarn. It was the only way to remain sane.

Gordon's stare drilled into Alfred. The old man scowled menacingly, its disgusting tongue slurping crudely across its pus cracked lips. A shriek! Gordon's feet moistened. Then a hand struck his neck.

That was the final straw! He threw caution to the wind and challenged the entity. 'Why the look!? What's the problem? Here! Talking to ya. Give it straight, old man?'

Instantly, the weird bird on the fence shrieked and disappeared into the thick darkness. 'Wretched bird! Stuff and nonsense' mumbled Gordon.

He refocused. 'Should be in bed, fella! Past bedtime in it?' The ghost gave an ominous grin, an evil expression transpired, and it approached methodically. Its features became young. Its countenance enlarged. Eye sockets hollow—and finally, it mutated into a hideous figure.

Gordon went for the torch. A flick of a switch. And a beam of light blasted onto the creature.

Dr Neilson sat in the hallway probing the TV monitors when instantly, his attention slinked to various electronic meters. Bizarre readings erupted! Crazy. Mad with intensity. Different audio needles and L.E.D. lights—synchronised.

The doctor's neck greased with sweat. He became excited. Thrilled. 'Gordon!' he cried. 'Quick! Here at once?' No sign. 'Where in the devil's name are you?'

Gordon shivered—gripped by fear. He shone his torch, not believing what he was witnessing. The entity had a rainbow-like outline, and its face portrayed death. Gordon's neck clicked. Then he turned before rampant evil in the air split the sky, ascending from the depths of hell.

'Doctor! It's started. Doctor Neilson!' implored Gordon. 'Quick. Something's here! HELP US! For the love of *GODDDDDDDDDDDDDDDD*!!!

Instantaneously, the entity materialized inches from my friend.

The bulb in the torch exploded, and a massive alien head—covered with orange light slammed into him. Gordon screamed, stretched out hands for protection, and curled into a ball. Knees pulled tight. Chest aching. Suddenly cracking electric sparks darted everywhere. Then, to conclude, a security light sprayed beams on the lawn from the neighbour's house.

Maria and I heard the 'scream' and dashed to the hallway.

Another scream rang out before I could utter a sentence, all-pervading with its terror and intensity. I gasped. Then peered at the front entrance.

Dr Neilson rose from his seat and threw away a microphone. He looked. Our eyes met in a hardened gaze. And our eyes knew! We knew a battle had begun. Started! The evil spirits had issued a challenge. A baleful purpose! Their menace had reared its ugly head. Eager to destroy us all.

'That shout. So, horrifying?' voiced Maria.

'A malevolent force! Thrown down the gauntlet,' said Dr Neilson. 'Instruments are reading activities. It's now or never. Stephen! We must confront the evil that's creeping. Stalking us.'

My courage fixed stern. I ran to the doorway. Dr Neilson trailed. For a moment, I stopped and glanced at Maria. 'Stay! Love. Don't move a muscle. Till we understand. What's going on?'

Maria agreed with a nod. The doctor and I exited and stood on the grass. We waited. Waiting for the shock. We observed. We searched the darkness as the moon winked with a menacing eye.

Then it unfolded. Gyrating and moving on the earth, Gordon fought something. Locked. Struggling. Violent convulsions were all-encompassing—the seizures hauling him side to side. While dirt, blood and grass smeared his clothes.

'Jesus!' I said, breathless. 'What the—'

'GET THIS THING OFF!' he yelled. 'TAKE IT OFFFFFFFFFFFF!!!.' Suddenly Gordon began fitting. Vomiting. Scratch marks from an invisible force tore apart his torso, and an orange light hovered—the same occurrence I'd witnessed when

Maria confronted the 'Alfred Personality.'

A gurgling transpired. Gordon lost consciousness. Moments turned into a lifetime. A nightmare-fuelled menace raised adjacent—it was the Alfred entity. Alone in a dark oppressing passageway. The corridor lengthened. Stretched. Beyond the eye. It then revolved. Next, a familiar voice recited religious guidance.

"If facing a demon on its own ground. Then the power from the exorcism ritual can defeat it. The demon is a liar! In its electronic domain. Gordon! Recite the ritual from GOD. Scream it! For all your life's worth."

Instantly, in the cold smoke, he traced the line of the Cross. Knelt on one knee. Bit his lip. Then his head sprang back when he unleashed the 'religious quotation.'

"God the Father commands you! God, the Son commands you!
The sacred Sign of the Cross commands you! The faith of the
Apostles commands you!
The blood of the Martyrs and the Saints command you! By the
living and the dead, I declare you depart from these servants of
GODDDDDDDDDDDDDDDDDD!!!"

This speech infuriated the dark *Spirit,* and, in an instant, the terrifying non-human entity attacked and then fired an unholy scream. 'Alfred is here! Who serves demons! In fire? For I AM A *MURDERERRRRRRRRRR!!!*'

'Arghaaaaaaaaaa,' cried Gordon.

Meanwhile, I'd noticed the orange illumination had vanished, but unfortunately, not my friend's epileptic fit.

'To hell with this! Wrench the lips!' I uttered. Panic within the words. 'Anything! Anything! Swallows his tongue. It's over! Jam something in the goddamn mouth!'

Dr Neilson gripped a screwdriver and butted the handle between Gordon's jaws.

I held on tight. Uncontrollable arms were everywhere. Then Gordon arched his back, curving into a contorted shape.

Suddenly, red fluid sprayed upon his chest. I threw a fist in my mouth. Bit it. Chewed it—until blood seeped from the knuckles. Disbelief enveloped us. I knew I had to use all my strength. Every effort. So I fell onto him and shoved a hefty arm round his neck.

'Can't hold!' I berated. 'Can't hold much longer.' I stared at Dr Neilson, begging! Needing a response.

'Drag the bastard! On the side!' gasped the big man. He thumped bruised palms onto Gordon's chest! Stabilising the situation. Swiftly, indoor lights flickered from the neighbour's house. I saw Carol peering through the patterned curtains. Thus, we had to drag Gordon into the hallway before she phoned the police.

Maria remained motionless. Locked still in the hallway. Despite the uproar unfolding. A look. There! She witnessed Dr Neilson restraining Gordon. She felt helpless. Hence, Maria threw caution aside and edged to the entrance.

However, silver sparks raised skywards from Dr Neilson's Diode machine. Maria halted. Gripped firm by suspense. She faced the electronic instruments! They raced. Brightened! And drew tiny flies to their shiny red lights—preparing the scene for a devilish performance.

And then it began. Bang! The sound vibrated the foundations. It happened again. BANG! And the entire house shook without mercy

Maria heard voices reverberating. At that moment, one of the video cameras eerily re-fixed. Changed direction. Creating loud whirling noises. She gazed aloft. Blue dots transpired! Next, orbs of mist manifested, and lastly, a glittery type of dust fell from upstairs.

Maria went distressed. Her voice dried. She found it tough to swallow saliva, and her mouth packed with dried grit.

'Hurry, Stephen,' she whispered fearfully. 'Please! Hurry!' Her desperate whispers centred in her distraught consciousness.

A howling wind emerged within the house. It travelled along the ceilings. The walls. Underneath the floorboards—followed by scratching. Gnawing. And scampering feet that split apart in the rafters of the house: Were rats in the attic?

Maria shivered. She glanced at one television. Blackness filled its screen. Then, inexplicably, it brightened. She shook her head slowly. Then, to her astonishment, a blurred face formed on the screen.

'God! No! NO!' she mumbled, straining on that ultimate term. The image on the interference-laden monitor grinned prior to melting within the snowy mush.

Outside, Gordon emerged from the fit. I hoisted him upright, and we hurried to the house.

Carol, outspoken and curt, dashed to the scene. Wanting answers! Wanting an explanation for events?

I made a phoney excuse, stating, 'Gordon was drunk and needed pills.' On the other hand, Dr Neilson yelled, 'Get lost!'

Enraged, she stormed into her house. I objected to the doctor's crass nature. However, there wasn't time to argue. I just wanted all of us safely in the house.

We struggled through the doorway and I slammed the makeshift door shut—progressing the hallway.

I noticed Maria. Tense and shaking like a leaf. So, I let Dr Neilson assist Gordon and rushed beside her. 'Trouble! What's wrong, honey?'

Maria's features whitened. Froze. She stared at the television. Then cast a glance. 'Stephen! Saw a *face!* On the *T V.*'

I shrugged. And peered at the television but only noticed dark pictures emanating from a video camera. Next, I examined an audio-visual machine—its indicators displayed 0000. Therefore, nothing—was recorded.

Gordon collapsed into a chair, jeans ripped, grey shirt torn and bloodied. To complete the misery, his battered expression resembled a corpse. Trickles of blood seeped from gashed lips— throaty breaths transpired, and he twitched and quivered.

To bring normality to proceedings, I clapped! And asked Maria, 'To fetch a glass of water?' She agreed and exited.

Meanwhile, Dr Neilson and I did a quick examination of Gordon. Trying to pinpoint any injuries—while he groaned incoherently and coughed gruffly.

Maria entered with a glass. She passed it to Gordon, his hands trembling. Then he drank the water in three gulps.

'What went on outside?' she asked.

'Wouldn't wanna know!' Diabolical encounters,' he replied. His voice was barely recognisable. 'Think I've gone mad! This entire business! Screwed us in the head.'

'Rational. Now! By chance. Know it's distressing,' probed Maria.

'I'm—' Gordon paused. Stammering his sentence. 'I—I'm... petrified. There's a thing. Alive in darkness! Within our fears. Seen it. It's something... something terrible.'

Dr Neilson interjected with a question fuelled with speculation. 'What did you observe? Paranormal forces arose. The readings on the oscilloscope indicated unearthly activity.'

'First of all,' replied Gordon. 'It, or whatever "it" was. Appeared to be an old man. Perfectly normal. Apart from one thing. The way it gravitated. Then I confronted it. A bad idea. Because a transfiguration occurred, the thing mutated into a hideous. Unspeakable entity! An adaptation of evil! Evil incarnate.'

Maria panicked. Nearly fainted. 'Oh my *God*! It's the same man!' Maria steered a terrified gaze. 'There's sickness here! We've gotta get out! Leave this dreadful place. Stephen! Before it's too—'

Swiftly, methodical thumps interrupted. Menace crept along the walls. Sinister shadows grew. Hulking! Maria shuddered as bangs quickened; their audibility was terrifying and nauseating.

I revolved clockwise. There! The disturbance came from the kitchen. I directed a stare. Bit my tongue while tension and anxiety turned my features ugly. '*Christ*!' I bellowed. 'Chaos has erupted. Tearing everything to pieces?'

'Kitchen!' replied Dr Neilson. 'Follow!'

Immediately, I trailed to the doorway. Then stopped. 'Maria, wait!' I demanded. 'Remain with Gordon. Be alert! Whatever it is! It's close!'

Next, I entered the kitchen. But for some unbeknown reason, everything went silent. Then, without warning, the electric cooker smashed. Uplifted and rocked violently by its own accord— followed by numerous plates and cups rising in the air and breaking against the tiled partitions.

'Poltergeist activity,' declared Dr Neilson. 'Haven't witnessed this type. Since the San Diego case. Circa 1981.'

'Poltergeist! A noisy spirit! Terrific!' Before I could utter anything else, a couple of knives ascended from the sink. Fixed in mid-air, then catapulted ahead, straight at the doctor and me.

'Watch it!' We both ducked, and the knives embedded into the grease-stained wall.

Dr Neilson steadied. And witnessed cupboards wrench off the fittings. Orange sparks followed. Like a fountain—burning pink and spreading upon the ceiling. I glanced aloft and noticed flames scorching various letters.

'See them. The words. Appearing,' I said.

'With complete distinction,' replied Dr Neilson.

Eventually, the phrase on the ceiling stated, *Mellissa Lives In The House*. I was aghast. Then, when about to speak, the fluorescent light blew up. And at that precise moment, something sprang upon my back, digging claws into the skin.

'Doctor! DOCTOR!' I yelled. 'Something's on us. What is it? WHAT THE HELL IS IT!!!'

The big man stared and deciphered the image. A yellow, orange light had shaped into the outline of a cat.

I flailed my arms. Beat fists on my back—anything to get the thing off.

'Believe it or not! A cat! Incredible! A full materialisation! Manifested with acute clarity. This is incredible.' Dr Neilson placed his hand on it. Then, however, the electric cooker crashed back, and angry flames arose.

The cat, or whatever it was jumped sideways, and I gripped the doctor's rough shoulder to beat a hasty retreat. 'We're outta here!' he exclaimed.

The unexplained disturbances strengthened, expelling us out of the kitchen. The door slammed, and the rattling cooker rammed tight against it.

Gordon and Maria remained in the hallway. They heard thumps. Cracks. Walloping thuds from the kitchen grew louder. Maria wanted to inspect the damage, but Gordon pulled her tight.

A chill transpired within the air. Maria shivered. The atmosphere changed. Changed into something cold and oppressive. She glanced at the different corners of the hallway. Expecting! Sensitive to fear. Then suddenly, all the noise from the kitchen ceased.

'Stay here! I beg! Please,' remarked Gordon.

Maria nodded. She readied for dialogue when Dr Neilson's electronic devices hummed—vibrated. And bizarre tones trailed. Then a video camera rattled on the staircase.

Maria shocked-still. Motionless. Rigid. An eerie stillness filtered through static clicks—emanating from the speakers. Gordon and Maria were afraid. Then one video camera exploded in a bright flash. They went terrified—clung to each other in fright, while gradually, pieces of the camera fell down the staircase.

Dr Neilson and I entered. The doctor noticed the electronic graph scribbling readings, and the oscilloscope and various instruments were in a frenzy.

I balanced beside Maria and Gordon, and we watched the unfolding events.

Instantly a loud burst of radio, white noise screeched from the doctor's Diode machine, and the imposing reel-to-reel tape machine powered On. He rushed to his chair and sat by the makeshift table.

All of us gathered. And that was the cue for Mellissa, the electronic ghost, to come through with its hissing, robotic voice. 'Good evening, Dr Andreas Neilson.' A deviant pause shrilled with interference and buzzing tones. 'Have you come to torment me?'

The doctor's confidence stirred. He barked a reply in an ancient dialect.

Gordon and I found this action perplexing.

Mellissa countered harshly. 'Ich… Liebe… Dich… Einer… Zimmer… Zim.'

My friend interrupted. 'What's it saying? It's German! Whas it mean?'

'Quiet!' scolded the doctor.

'Fruchbar! Fruchbar!' Mellissa pronounced. 'Where I inhabit. People rejoice. Glory in pain. We live. I am reborn. Stephen! I'm in the house. Standing near. Feel us! Let me tease you!' Suddenly, a sensation like that from a tongue slithered along my neck. 'Shit!' Then I shivered. 'Doctor! Something licked me! This whole damn charade… is outta control. It's ghosts at the windows. Demons in the attic. Waiting to strike!'

Dr Neilson reacted. 'Let me be the judge of that. I'm a man of science. An exorciser of ghosts.'

With all the events manifesting in the house, I became justifiably annoyed.

I dabbed my neck with a handkerchief, and Maria grasped us tight, squeezing my hand. Thus, the temper eased, and frustration faded.

Mellissa asked further questions, but the doctor didn't reply. His course of action enraged the ghost or entity. 'You will answer!' it demanded.

All of us remained silent. Finally, the hissing robotic voice roared, 'ANSWER ME!'

'I will not!' replied Dr Neilson. At that point, he counterattacked. 'You have no right! To be here… Exist on this earthbound plane. I command you! And other presences. Depart to the spiritual bridge. Cross over! And end the intrusion of this earthbound spiritual sphere.' Then, a few audible sounds resembling a demon hissed, *Wolfgang Peterson Is Here.*'

The doctor dismissed the statement with contempt. 'My friend's dead! Don't impersonate him! Hold the lies. Go languish with the earthbound spirits. Retreat, Mellissa I—I… co—command you.'

The last sentence Dr Neilson uttered had a core of indecision. A foolish thing—as immediately his face suffered a blow from an invisible hand, sending him spinning backwards and out of his chair. I, Maria, and Gordon knelt, 'You hurt?' I asked.

The doctor barged us aside and yelled, 'Be it by God. Or force of will! I command you to leave this place! Or I'll drive you to hell.'

Chillingly, we heard a massive charge of electrical energy rip-roar from the Diode machine, and a tirade of words explode. 'PERCEIVE I ANDREAS NEILSON!' screamed Mellissa. Its phrase packed with hate. 'And your compatriots! Those rancid compatriots who defy the spirits of the frequency domain!'

We all shuddered. Then gazed transfixed at the Diode machine. Mellissa's voice erupted. Hateful. Arising into an earth-shattering cry. 'You will all die! We come through the infinite ASTRAL TIMESTREAM.' A brief silence halted proceedings before one last ear penetrating scream ensued. 'You'll perish! PERISH!!! AND ALL! Die! *DIEEEEEEEEEEEEEEE!!!*'

Dr Neilson struggled, whacked the Diode machine, and then ripped the plug from the socket. Thus, cutting the power.

Suddenly, loud thumps split at a distance. Ramping pressure cracked the walls. And bangs sequenced into blows.

The disturbance came from upstairs. Dr Neilson arose and pushed past—edging his way to the bottom of the staircase. Set to ascend the steps and head to the malevolent workshop.

I thought this crazy. Not the right course of action. This man seemed incompetent. Unable to control the paranormal chaos energizing throughout the house. Maria released her hand from my grip and trailed the doctor. He turned. Then made frantic arm gestures. 'Stop!'

She stared at his bearded face, noticing a massive red *mark* where the invisible hand struck.

'Mrs Reid,' voiced the doctor. 'Do not come! Stay!' Next, he uttered instructions. 'Gordon. Observe and check the electronic instruments. They are our only defence against evil forces. We must be in unity! So, dissect the exact readings—outputted. No power's in the Diode machine. Therefore, no spirit voices can enter.'

I stepped forward. 'That's bullshit! The spirits don't need a frickin' Diode machine. They're initiating contact from another source. A different realm—another goddamn energy structure.'

'Don't defy science! Or question motives. I know what I'm doing! Nothing can harm you.'

'Rubbish! Absolute nonsense,' I began. 'Christ almighty. What about your face? Took a punch from an unseen force.'

Gordon intervened. 'Stephen's right! You're out of your depth. Arsehole!'

Instantly, Dr Neilson gripped his throat. And both knocked against the staircase before brawling on the floor.

Maria screamed. 'Stop it! PLEASE!!!'

Somehow I separated them. Then, in an air of unreality and madness, we argued with one another. Screaming. Berating.

Abruptly, the fiery altercation ceased when a thunderous crash shook the house's foundations and emitted damp earth from the garden.

'Listen! Listen to me!' exclaimed the doctor. 'We're doing precisely what this ghost Mellissa… and the other entities want. It's up to us to banish the evil forces. They're growing stronger. Prevailing in authority by the hour. Ready for the final attack! They feed off doubts and emotions. Stephen and I. Must confront the beast. The demon. Now!'

'Don't! Don't go upstairs?' begged Maria, forebodingly, 'I'm afraid. For all our sakes.'

Dr Neilson punched the chair in frustration. He removed a gadget from his pocket and demanded silence.

It was then serious concerns arose. Encircling me with distrust. Dr Neilson seemed ill-judged. Reckless. I think he had not experienced this kind of violent paranormal activity. No matter how qualified he claimed to be.

Chapter Thirteen

Gordon's feelings urged him to escape the house and go to another location before disaster enveloped everyone.

Maria agreed. Thus, Gordon directed the 'point' at Dr Neilson, but he dismissed it. Nothing could dampen his ego. He didn't want advice because he had pride in what he was undertaking and had prepared himself to confront the paranormal force head-on.

Grave doubts ate within us. I feared something dreadful could unfold. But unfortunately, no amount of persuasion could prevent the big man from his mission.

I glimpsed at Maria, hiding apprehension. 'My dear! Let's get a cab! Won't take long. Then you stay in a hotel. Only for one night. Things are deep. Dangerous here!' I added. 'You've been through enough!'

Maria went stubborn. 'Sorry, love. Not gonna happen. If I leave. Then you leave. Comprehend!'

'Gordon!' I begged. 'Take her to yours. For the—'

'He can't—!' finished Dr Neilson. 'Equipment needs maintaining. The electronic graph reader checked—and video cameras readied—to catch unearthly activity!'

I demanded a 'private conversation' with Gordon. Grudgingly, the doctor agreed.

I told my friend if things deteriorated—he would take Maria and head to a place of safety.

Abruptly, the doctor interjected. 'Move it. Stephen! Come on!' Gradually he ascended the staircase—while holding an electronic indicator device.

I tapped my mate on the arm and wagged a *finger.* 'Remember!' Then, unsteadily, I went to the stairs.

However, Maria tugged my shirt. 'Stephen. You're not going with the doctor. Something's amiss! Wrong! I don't trust him!'

My brow creased. 'I created this evil… On a scale from one to ten. Paranormal events—are at ten! Now! I've guarded faith in the guy. Even if he's eccentric.' I embraced Maria, kissed her, and backed away.

'Stephen!' rasped Dr Neilson, rising the staircase. 'Here!'

I briefly remained at the bottom rung before ambling a few hesitant steps. Then I progressed and quickened, eager to accompany the doctor to the staircase's summit.

A minute later, we both stood on the landing—with only a dim light glowing—a faulty lamp, the culprit.

My eyes scanned nervously. Everything quiet. The beatings were gone, and events were quite ordinary under the circumstances.

However, relief was unwise, as the doctor's electronic instrument short-circuited. He threw it to the floor in despair. At that precise moment, we heard directly ahead the sound of shuffling. Or movement of soft shoes. It seemed like a spiritual force had slippers at its disposal, but nothing visible emerged.

In the gadget-filled hallway, Gordon sat, studying the television monitors. Finally, he curved to the floor and adjusted one of the main auxiliary cables.

Maria stepped up and squinted her eyes—when they caught sight of the screens.

Unexpectedly, one of the television's pictures flashed. Snowy interference arose, and beaming lines scrolled erratically. Maria re-focused and deciphered Dr Neilson and I. Balanced on the landing. Then thick snowy interference assimilated the picture.

Gordon busied himself twisting one firm cable. He cursed and eventually fixed it in place.

Maria peered at the other television, and through the black mush, a transfiguration started—changing into an unspeakable thing. Then, abruptly, she tapped Gordon's shoulder.

'Problem?' he remarked as he jolted upright.

Maria pointed. 'What's that?' she uttered, voice cracking. 'The ghostly face. Witnessed it earlier?'

Gordon edged to the monitor. Eyes widened with astonishment. The supernatural image developed with defining clarity—resembling a woman. Maria threw a trembling hand against her mouth.

Gordon shocked! 'You two!' he gasped aloft. 'One camera! Got something!'

'By God, man! What's position!' barked Dr Neilson. 'It's on the monitor. State its form?'

Gordon studied the image. An evil grin transpired before it obscured and blurred out of focus.

Then he noticed a hand twitching six odd-looking fingers in an *unknown sign*. Next, the television picture cleared, revealing the woman's eerie features. She mouthed word-like pronunciations from the lips in a slow, mechanical fashion.

'JESUS! A woman!' shrieked Gordon. 'Face of a woman.' His following words erupted. 'My *God*! Ahead of ya!'

I stepped forward, waited—and stared into the dim light. I whispered. 'Can't see a damn thing!'

Swiftly, the window by the landing cracked. Rattled! And split—accompanied by slams and hissing voices originating from the workshop.

'Don't like this,' I moaned. 'Let's make a break for it!'

Maria went emotional. 'Stephen! She's there! Believe us! The thing's on the screen.' My wife's eyes drew to the ghost before the image dissipated into the mush of television interference.

'Shit! It's gone!' raged Gordon as he adjusted the brightness. 'Whatever it was. Vanished. Into thin air.'

On the landing, the doctor and I tried to perceive the apparition. When suddenly, everything went quiet. And only unnerving silence transpired. The oppression and drama of the situation made my body ache and cramp and burn with pain. Yet the worst awaited. Ready to flush the scene with evil.

Before I could say a thing, glittering dust appeared high in the air. It brightened the whole landing with a spooky snowy light. I watched in disbelief. Amazed. Astounded at what was unfolding. 'Explanation, doctor? You're the expert!'

Dr Neilson gazed in wonder. He removed his spectacles and put them on to get a defined view. 'No idea, Stephen. Seen nothing like this in thirty-two years. So, bang goes experience! Research!' He bowed aside. 'Are you receiving this phenomenon?' he bellowed. 'Downstairs?'

Gordon gazed inflexibly at a monitor. Flicked switches. Pushed buttons on the panel. Anything to gain diverse camera angles. Yet, no matter what he adjusted—nothing appeared.

Maria's eyes steered to another television. She was desperate to catch the shapes that eluded Gordon, but she didn't witness any occurrence.

Gordon yelled breathlessly. 'I'm getting absolutely… NOTHING. FRICKIN' SOD ALL!'

Upon the landing, both of us held rigidly—transfixed by this fearsome luminosity. Suddenly, the bright, glittery dust reformed. Creating a shape. It brightened and gradually materialised into a beautiful, angelic woman.

I glanced at Dr Neilson—wanting reassurance. Desperate for a solution. But he languished on another planet. Frozen to the spot. Observing in amazement, the paranormal display evolving without notice.

I re-focused on the mysterious figure. Then it began. Quiet

clicking noises arose in the left ear. And I felt an invisible force drag us headfirst.

My breathing reduced. Faintness enveloped. And I lost control as if a kind of hypnotic trance had taken me over.

The strange, ghostly figure beckoned. Teased! Tormented! The clicking sound in the ear increased. Intensified. And an audible pop exploded in my head as something supernatural flashed across my eyes. I wanted out—to flee the house. Yet the force held me tight! Motionless. Unable to move in either direction.

I knew this evil paranormal thing desired us. I became devoid of pain. Could not feel a pinprick—not even Dr Neilson's rigid finger. Digging. Pointing! Eager to release us from this ungodly trance.

The doctor was shocked—frightened to the point of death—for only the second time. The other, escaping the Amazonian Indians on the ill-fated Major Gregory Phillips' expedition.

Dr Neilson searched for ideas. *Quick! Break the link*, he thought. Instantly, he hauled me back. At that moment, a hard whack, prior to a fist. Pounded. All-pervading—slamming into his jaw.

The doctor stumbled. Blood distended the eyes. Then his spectacles shattered and fell aside. He thrashed his arms defensively—anything to prevent the invisible force's attack.

However, lightning *blue flashes* flared from Inner Space and the invisible void—the void that surrounds us in time and dimensions.

Maria shouted. Waiting—frantic for an answer. Dr Neilson attempted to answer. But a mighty hand thumped his mid-rift— followed by relentless punches.

He doubled up and then directed an order. 'Stephen! No! Don't! Provoke, it!'

Suddenly, all the video cameras upon the staircase glowed and rattled.

Maria rushed to the bottom stair. '*STEPHENNNNN!!!*'

At that instant, I heard several electrical booms—like scattergun blasts.

Bright electrical flashes trailed, and Maria hurried to Gordon, watching the television monitors; he jolted back, gazing in agonising torment at the unfolding events. His breaths turned raw.

Then sweat greased Gordon's brow when he yelled that fateful cry as the cameras exploded—unleashing bright flames. Packing the darkness with demonic terror. *I'VE LOST ALL THE PICTURES!!!'*

Maria screeched. *'FOR GOD'S SAKE!* We have got to get out! GET OUT OF HERE!'

The next-door neighbour, Carol, dashed onto the porch while a crowd of citizens stood adjacent, woken by the bangs and commotion. Gathering—restless and nosey.

Echoes turned into agony when an encore of explosions pitched to the heavens. Like mighty cannons firing in a fury.

Carol glanced at John in the doorway, and their eyes met. He knew. She knew. And John feared someone shot—that Maria and I lay dead.

Immediately, he dialled the police. At the Station, a clerk took the call and initiated 'an armed response' team to investigate the scene.

****

Dr Neilson lunged desperately on the landing to force me down—slam me to the floor. He reached out. But before I could take a grip, a blinding spectral light burst free from the angelic apparition—its diabolical energy passed straight through us.

I rotated like a figurine before being catapulted ahead. Then, I came to rest on the carpet floor—blood tricking from my lips. Finally, I lost consciousness. Unaware of events igniting everywhere.

Another ball of light erupted from the apparition, thumping into Dr Neilson. *'ARGHHHHHHHH!'* he yelled frantically, throwing fists at his eyes to prevent blindness.

Gordon and Maria yelled. Cried! Berated! Pleading that all of us had to flee.

An invisible hook-type claw gripped the doctor round the throat—trying to tear out the larynx. The grip and force intensified. Driving him rearwards. He tried with all strength and weight to fight the power, but something yanked his waist—causing a levitation effect.

Then Mellissa's voice established. Whispering creepily. 'Dr Neilson. You left Wolfgang Peterson. To die! He suffers in torment due to your selfish actions. Your pathetic bravado. Engaged! During the Phillips expedition.'

'Untruthful bastard!' rebuked the doctor. 'Be gone, unclean spirit. I demand it! Leave this place and return to the domain of sick. Voracious! Damnation! Bury yourself in the sphere of malevolence! Where frustrated demons sow discourse against God!'

Mellissa hissed like the devil. And a massive thunder flash drove from its centre, slamming into the doctor. He grasped the stair railing, trying to hold on. Yet, blood greased his fingers—and his grip failed before he whirled upon the window.

Dr Neilson's heartfelt scream turned into my name. '*STEPHENNNNNNNNNNNNN!*' Instantly, he crashed through the shattered glass and hit the ground outdoors with a thump.

Thunderous vibrations and massive explosive booms smashed sections of the walls. Creating spiralling cracks that rose throughout the house—pictures and lumps of plaster split, chipped into chunks, and fell to the floor like tumbling tombstones abused by bulking demons.

Gordon had witnessed enough. He enacted my warning—violent events were beyond control.

'Maria,' he growled. 'We're gone! The front door. Get to it. *GOOOOOOO!!!*' He rose from a chair, and his eyes picked a spot! There! A key was hanging in the door lock.

Then suddenly, a light hovered above his head, blue lightning flashes followed, and to conclude, a high-pitched buzzing erupted—the audible levels deafening. He threw hands over his head. Yelled in pain and staggered as if a ghoulish creature were atop his shoulders. He peered at the electronic panel before many amber and yellow lights struck, slashing his face with welts and cuts.

'MARIA!!!' yelled Gordon. 'Cover your eyes. Don't look at the lights! Run! *RUNNNNNNN!!!*'

Her terrified gaze steered to Gordon. She saw wounds, bleeding profusely. Then, abruptly, the buzzing altered into whispering voices and one television screen split. Blinding electrical smoke arose. Vented—next, a hideous voice basked in evil roared for retribution.

Maria screamed. Went for Gordon. Pulling his arm. Panicking. Anything so they could both reach the door. Subsequently, a thing prickled her neck. The ticking from watches changed into murmurs, and a shaft of blue dust manifested, convoyed with a 'ghostly scream.' Its force lifted Maria off the floor and sent her rolling through thin air before she lost consciousness.

Gordon freaked! Shouted and bawled—and the other television blew up.

An object exploded from the tape recorder, igniting into flames, striking a blow. Gordon clutched his chest, descended to his knees, and collapsed.

Dr Neilson lay on the ground outside—body peppered with glass—blood dripping from his mouth.

John and Carol hurried to the scene. John clenched the doctor's wrist. Checking for sign of life.

'Damn! Can't feel a pulse.' He performed mouth to mouth. It didn't work. So he thumped the chest. First with one fist. Then two. Anything to restart the heart.

Other people gathered in morbid fascination. Their heads rose toward the thumping windows. There! They bore witness to amber flashes, the windows awash with blue orbs, and the outer walls separating from snaking cracks eating into the brickwork.

John hauled Dr Neilson onto his side—to clear the airway.

Restart breathing. However, it was futile—Dr Neilson lay dead.

Carol shuddered. Face trembling. Heart racing. 'How long! How quick?' she said. 'Will it take for the police?'

'An armed response team's on the way! Be here. Shortly.' John coughed. Trembled—and wiped mud and glass from his brow. Next, he removed a handkerchief and dabbed aside the blood—on the doctor's face.

Without warning, ear-penetrating echoes reverberated within the house. 'Listen! Carol!' he exclaimed. 'Get away?' He turned his attention to the small crowd. 'For *Christ sake!* People. Go home!'

In the distance, a wail of sirens transpired. Naturally, therefore, police vans and cars approached.

On the landing, I lay dazed and motionless. I tried to speak but could only murmur incoherently. I felt light-headed and surreal. Then, gradually, my sore eyes narrowed open. Pain existed everywhere. My chest ached. Like a wound rubbed with salt. My complexion had turned ashen—body drenched in sweat. Lastly, I noticed the smashed landing window encased in a thick greenish mist.

I cried for Maria. For Gordon. However, no reply. Then I knew I had to hoist myself up and try to escape.

Before I could catch breath, directly ahead, the ghostly apparition's colour altered—changing into darkish red. A mist transpired. Thick. Nauseating. I gripped the carpet and gazed aloft. Then, a dark figure materialised—replacing the angelic figure.

Outside, commotion increased when the screech of tyres brought several cars to a standstill. Five police cars and an armed response van halted. Rapidly four heavily armed men exited their van, and police colleagues stepped aside. Heated exchanges fixed and fired with expletives, and the police shoved everybody— truncheons drawn—driving back the locals.

A makeshift yellow-taped cordon was firmly erected and drawn across the driveway—sealing off the scene.

I heard shouting! Voices. Commands. Accompanied by droning sirens, but these were the least of my concerns. I noticed the dark figure had fully materialised between flares of luminosity—outlined like a woman. Sprinkled with a glittery stardust material.

It began disappearing and reappearing every time it graced closer. I knew whatever it was—sought revenge.

'Stay back! Torment another!' I raged. 'Be it done! Finished! Can't you see! What more do you want? YER HEAR ME! THE GAME'S OVER!'

A foul smell filtered through the air. Its unpleasant aroma like that of decaying eggs. My stomach wrenched. Heaved. Then I vomited bile and saliva until I sobbed with pain.

Suddenly, the ghostly figure appeared only inches away. I noticed it was devoid of legs—floating upward—soaring with shuddering power and a horrific presence.

Next, two black, leathery hands passed over us. My whole body quivered. Shook. Next, a forceful grip strengthened. Dragging me in the air. I threw fists to battle the supernatural figure, but it felt as if a material-type cloth ripped apart when I did this action.

A massive white flash entered, and I arose from the ground—slamming face to face against the thing hovering opposite.

Then I knew! Knew exactly. Who this terrifying apparition was.

'You.' I said, pausing in shock before I uttered the name fixed within me. 'You're, Mellissa.'

'How clever. Dr Einstein,' it hissed, voice echoing into tortured cries. 'Stephen Reid! I no longer require inferior machines. Can attack the living without electronics. My authority's all-pervading. And cannot be stopped!' On those words, its head flung back, and it rip-roared a hideous laugh. Visions of death manifested. And after the laughter faded, it exalted triumphantly—blitzing the scene with terror.

That was the cue for an unearthly wind to envelop the landing and rock the house.

Inside of us, fury and insanity peaked to a climax. I screamed. Raged and in a blind show of destructive anger—wrapped hands upon the neck of Mellissa. Next, hysteria ensued, and I released a bellowing roar. 'YOU WORTHLESS… *BITCHHHHHHHHH*!'

I followed up with a forceful blow. Elbows. Fists. Anything to fight the entity. But instantly, Mellissa's leathery arms clamped around my wrist. I cried before it snapped because of Mellissa's evil deeds.

The entity's hollow face enlarged—mutated and salivated with sickening lust.

I heard a police officer speaking through a loudhailer, asking all occupants to leave the house.

Mellissa's façade morphed into something chilling and grotesque. I tried striking out, despite intense agony, due to a bone protruding from my wrist.

I urgently needed to escape, but this non-human entity seemed hell-bent on killing us.

Outside the house, police officers dressed in riot gear—and the armed attack unit had guns poised to shoot. Another police car screeched to a halt, and four plain-clothed detectives exited. John, who remained close to the taped cordon, advised them not to enter the house with guns.

A tense conversation ensued between him and Detective Hawkings. 'Reported this incident! Correct, sir?'

'Yeah,' replied John, gazing at an ambulance rolling into view. 'Something's wrong. In my neighbour's house.'

'What's his name?'

'Stephen Reid.'

John's attention drifted. He noticed green-suited paramedics in the driveway rotating Dr Neilson on a stretcher. Hawkings looked on as the doctor's battered body passed.

A medical assistant glanced at John, then shook his head despondently. Next, the medics hurried onward.

Another police officer pleaded for people in the house to 'leave', or they'd force entry. Hawkings noted events. 'Know if your neighbour,' he asked. 'Mr Reid. Possessed firearms. Kept any in the house?'

'No way! Never! Haven't seen him with weapons,' countered John. 'Definitely not! Had no interest in guns. Would've told us otherwise. However, an incident occurred—few days ago. When his wife. Went crazy. Continuously screaming inside the house. Stephen assumed a home invasion. An intruder!' Added John. 'Got in somehow. We forced the door. And searched for the assailant—but there was no evidence. Nothing! To confirm an intruder. I searched the house from tip to toe.'

Hawkings readied a remark when a multitude of thunderbolts powered at the armed police in quick succession.

'Incoming! Hold your fire!' shouted an officer. 'Someone's shooting!' Instantly, police car windscreens shattered, sending splinters of glass everywhere.

****

Mellissa's grip tightened—squeezed, and I lost all consciousness.

Suddenly the workshop door burst open, and all my equipment violently ejected. Acrid smoke followed, emitting suffocating fumes.

Mellissa's face attained its sick profile. Horror within the smile. I tried a final despairing yell before its black leathery hands drew blood from the neck.

Abruptly, a massive blue flash enlightened the scene. Roars from evil spirits massed upon the area—and finally, my Diode machine exploded into fire.

The blue flash caused a deafening bang. Erupting! Devastating! With its intensity. The windows of the house shattered. Pieces of glass and debris hit the assembled people and the police officers. An officer with a gun stumbled and hit the ground, while women screamed and panicked.

Maria lay dead still. Then slowly, breath moistened her lips. Finally, her eyes flickered, and she aroused to consciousness.

She witnessed mist arising from the electronic equipment and noticed Gordon unconscious a few feet away. Consequently, she rose disjointedly, with vision blurring.

Noises from the attack by Mellissa stung her ears. Instantly, any power in the house ceased, rolling thunderclaps followed, and streaking flashes balled into darting orbs.

Then a disturbing scene unveiled. Bodily shapes manifested. The dead wandered the hallway as aimless refugees. Not knowing why they were summoned to this earthly place before a hideous electronic buzzing took them back to the "City of the Dead."

'Stephen! Help!' cried Maria as she collapsed to the floor. Subsequently, an upturned cable fastened tight on her ankles, the paranormal force within the house was preparing to kill her.

The 'call' from Maria distracted Mellissa. Then, its grip faltered, and it threw me to the ground.

I felt enormous pressure push on my back; it felt as if a large woman sat astride. Next, her entire body slammed atop. A massive smack sliced marks on cheeks, and blood gushed from welts. I gasped. Stifled breaths. Then felt myself dragged—forced in the direction of the shattered window.

I tried clutching the bannister, but my grip loosened due to smeared blood.

I knew the only chance for survival lay in time. If I could hold on. Surely someone would arrive. Free us from the evil beast. I waited. Strained and hoped. Desperate for anyone to enter.

Bang! The damaged front door split apart. Policemen crashed into the house, torches raised, dressed in riot gear, and screaming 'orders.'

Maria shrieked. Three policemen approached. Then yanked her rearwards as raging fires emitted flaking cinders.

Another officer directed a torch at Gordon. Motionless—resting on the floor, semi-conscious. Body covered in pieces of wire and rolls of tape.

Maria tugged at the police officer. 'PLEASE! GOD! IT'S

STEPHEN! MY HUSABAND! He's upstairs. You Gotta get him. The ghosts want us dead!'

A policeman and his colleague dashed to the staircase. Shone dazzling torches aloft, and their eyes fixed. There! In the fog, they deciphered a *dark image* smiling overhead the stairway. It was Mellissa. They thought it was me. And with ignorance clouding judgment, they raged, 'Mr Reid! 'FOLLOW US! HOUSE IS READY TO BURN!' Then, with bated breaths, they hastened onto the steps.

Suddenly, a force sent me spinning at the shattered window. The thick solid mist parted, and I keeled over, clipping my hip on the side of the buckled window frame. It tossed us aside, and I hit a tree beside the house.

Shocked shouts from a crowd of onlookers erupted when the tree broke my fall. I pulled knees to the chest—squinted my eyes. And clenched fists tight when I slammed on the damp earth with a sickening thump.

Back within, the image of Mellissa faded from view—ahead of the policemen.

Instantly, both police officers' torches exploded, and a forked beam enlightened where Mellissa once stood, driving them back.

Maria tried to escape a burly police officer. Then began screaming.

Suddenly smoke emitted from upstairs, and one of the television monitors in the hallway exploded. Hawkings turned to a colleague. 'GET OUT AT ONCE!'

Outdoors John gestured at Maria—observing me lying injured on the grass.

The police officers in the house managed to drag Gordon aloft and heave him through the main entrance. At that moment, the hallway flared into fires, and thick charred smoke poured from the kitchen.

Chapter Fourteen

I rolled aloft in distress and groaned in pain. My hip hurt immensely, and I saw a paramedic examining an oxygen mask from the corner of my eye.

Diverse voices from strangers established within the eardrums, and I gasped for breath and coughed up blood.

People of authority peppering the scene were frantic. Breathless. As for me, I feared death drawing upon us. Maria rushed onward and witnessed me lying on the ground.

In emotional turmoil, she ran to her husband, pushing various people aside, knelt slowly and placed her gentle hand on my forehead, taking care not to delay the paramedics—working on the injuries.

A few people jostled one another as Maria kissed us softly.

Gordon, dazed and confused, barged a passage through the mob and went to her. He glanced at the house—an almighty fire had taken hold—devoid of mercy.

My friend threw a palm to his eyes, bowed his head and sobbed profoundly due to stress.

A fire engine wailed in the distance. At the same time, a crowd of onlookers shoved and murmured with concern while John and Carol quarrelled fervently with police officers.

Abruptly, a detective barked commands. 'Will you guys clear the area? This isn't a show. There's no last act!'

Another bang vented in a fury—chaos ensued, and people fought and panicked. Then, behind Maria, the fire exploded. It was unrestrained and widespread. She removed her hand from my head and gazed at the burning home—furious flames rose out the roof. 'Stephen! Oh, Stephen!' she wept. 'Our future's gone! Up in smoke. We're gonna lose everything!'

At that moment, I lost breath, and my taxed lungs filled with blood trickles. Next, I passed out, and all the pain and noise disappeared.

I found myself in a bluish mist; the surroundings resembled a medieval chapel, enlightened with burning lanterns.

'Is anyone there?' I asked.

In a flash, a woman appeared, wearing a twelfth-century hooded robe. Her long black hair was awash with curls—pointing from the brown hood. She was tall and slim, and her age was twenty-five.

'Where the hell am I?' I asked.

She put her hands together as if to pray, and then her eyes closed. They met mine when she opened them, and black eye sockets emerged. 'You are here with us… Stephen.'

'What do you mean? Here with us,' I said in fear. The burning red lanterns immediately cut, and all that remained in their place were puffs of smoke.

I fathomed I was dead. For to see a vision like this is beyond comprehension—beyond consciousness. And beyond the realms of human life.

Then an enormous array of busy lights became apparent, and I entered a gigantic auditorium, like a theatre. However, it had remarkable white fountains of luminosity rising and falling in the background.

Massive silk sheets. Bleached and peppered with blazing sparks fluttered. Hanging in the air—as if watching me. Yet this place wasn't a theatre.

Then, abruptly, the colour of the entire scene waxed white and went pallid. And next, it dawned. For I realised I stood in some kind of imposing laboratory.

Conversations from various Celestial Beings started, detailing reference points. They resembled Greek Gods. Gathering and discussing with one another—all-pervading with fantastic knowledge.

Their sphere was not of our physical earth. Instead, it was a parallel dimension—one of the Astral World's Realms. It was described by ancient religions, spiritualist circles, and dabblers of the Occult as the place where the dead went after they passed on.

I voyaged onward and graced amongst figures dressed in silver coats. They resembled scientists. Then I noticed strange machines, like giant computer systems.

I approached, and a voice spoke. 'Friend! Welcome. To the Astral Timestream. A station where we communicate with the higher planes of existence. Where only the kind souls reside, our technicians instigate communications with electronic devices. Harness genuine conversations. Not false ones from the lying demons. Look over there, friend. Observe citizens who aid us in our detailed work.'

There! I noticed famous people from past centuries. Prominent writers. Leaders and talented individuals—their lives documented in humankind's books and movies.

I wanted to explore—to research this arena of spirits. Become a part of it forever, and be at peace. But suddenly, and oh so terribly, breaths failed. I clutched my chest—and crumpled to my knees as if struck by a forceful hammer.

I looked toward the dark floor—then a colossal pressure forced us on a descent. Finally, lightness faded, and I rotated in complete darkness.

Suddenly a horrendous pressure on the ribs transpired, and I cried in pain. In desperation!

A blue-purple light manifested through the darkness, which I seemed destined to arrive. Nevertheless, as I travelled closer, two images raised to their feet.

There! Stood Dr Andreas Neilson. He implored. Berated! Beseeched! 'Stephen, stay afar! This dimension's manipulated for evil. Hitler's here. Other despicable figures rejoice. They lurk in the electronic shadows. Using spirit transmission stations to curse the living. But Stephen! And for the love of *God*! Your antagonist lives! She's here. Look!'

To my horror, Mellissa nestled alongside. *I* knew I would be *dead* if I continued the descent. A spooky glow surrounded us. Dr Neilson threw out his arm—I grabbed it.

'Hold on,' he cried. '*HOLD ONNNNNN*!!!'

I gripped tight. The descent stopped. And I heard Mellissa's voice, 'Rebuke us.'

In an instant, the entity edged behind Dr Neilson and gripped his shoulders between black, leathery hands. The doctor's grasp failed—and Dr Neilson fell—managing one last instruction.

'Save yourself. Your soul. Go to the light! GO INTO THE *LIGHTTTTTTTTT*!!!'

The remnants of the doctor's spirit body—energy formation—reared back and vanished into a gloomy mist.

I began drifting upwards at tremendous speed. Lastly, I entered a dark tunnel, and a magnificent window of blinding light manifested ahead.

I saw a sparkling blue light with many arms emerging—following at speed. A murky, hollow face popped out of the blue spectral light. It was Mellissa. I gazed back at the white radiance and saw my father—and other relatives.

Then 'Alfred', the old man I had known all those years ago, stepped forward. '*... Time Is The Essence... For The Rest Of My Duties.*' His words squared together in staggered delay echoes.

'Alfred! All of ya!' I cried. 'Send us back! To the Astral Timestream. A place of science. A place of wonder!'

The *sentence* from Alfred repeated once more. Before white light enveloped and I felt the life force drain away.

Suddenly a tremendous pain ripped across my head, a blinding silver light shadowed me, and I heard voices uttering medical terms.

I gasped, breathed, and stirred from unconsciousness—a massive jolt directed into the chest. My aching eyes peeled open, and then I realised! I lay on a hospital bed in an Accident and Emergency Department. Doctors and Nurses were frenetic. Injecting different drugs to keep us alive. They dabbed the face. Then an oxygen mask hit my paling features.

At that moment, I witnessed to the left my darling, Maria. I gripped one of the doctor's jackets. 'Please don't let me perish,' I begged. 'Maria will die! Broken-hearted. For love is our bond! A bond that strengthens with desire!'

'Stephen! Remain stable,' replied a doctor. 'Relax. Breathe. We'll make you comfortable. Okay.'

A nurse hooked a monitor to my chest—checking heartbeats. I gripped the nurse, glanced right—and felt a chill scratch along the neck.

Maria went to us, and our hands squeezed firm. 'Stephen! Stay with me! I love you! I LOVE YOU!'

Crack! A rib snapped before a doctor injected adrenalin. Mellissa, whose appearance seemed invisible to everyone, glided to the side of the bed, barging Maria aside. My wife hit the hospital floor. Then Mellissa's leathery arm gripped the chest.

'Can you see the ghost? CAN YOU SEE IT!' I screamed. The doctors shook their heads in dismissal

I gritted teeth. Then, with almighty strength and fortitude, I unleashed a final tirade that split the atmosphere and destroyed the entity. 'DEPART THIS REALM! GOD IS POWER! END THIS, MELLISSA! RETURN TO THE WORLD OF... *EVPPPPP!*'

Before I lost consciousness, the last thing I remember was a massive blast of light. A mysterious crash. Whispering voices. Before everything vanished into an explosion of ethereal light— concluding this grand finale.

Gradually my condition improved. Therefore, by a miracle, the medical staff had saved my life. I remembered nothing else until I came round a few hours later in the recovery room. Later, I noticed police officers at the bedside during different intervals.

The loving appearance of Maria arrived—however, I would drift in and out of sleep for the resulting hours.

Epilogue

The weeks that followed were traumatic for me, Gordon and Maria. All of us questioned meticulously about those terrifying events on the night of the disturbance.

The fire and the death of Dr Andreas Neilson gave the police something to focus on, though we stuck to the 'same story.' We had to—as it was the truth.

A detailed investigation by detectives established no connections. And an inquest held into the doctor's demise made the coroner conclude:

Dr Neilson's Death Caused By Misadventure and not Manslaughter.

The police continued gunning for leads and responses and refused to believe witness statements. Therefore, they charged us with various offences.

The only 'Facts' that could strengthen our defence would have emerged from video camera recordings on that fateful night.

But mysteriously, the only camera which survived recorded nothing of relevant value.

The prosecution was furious as they did not have enough detailed evidence—a watertight solid case, and we escaped with the minor sentence of Community Service and Fines.

I felt relieved but slightly disturbed. I blamed myself for the death of the doctor. It would always prey on the mind, as with other unworldly matters.

****

Nine months passed, and the police closed the case. This lifted an enormous burden that hung over Maria and me. After that, however, misfortune shadowed Gordon, as his Electrical Store ceased trading due to negative publicity. He subsequently left the country to stay with relatives in France—so we did not see him again after the police investigation.

As for Maria and me, we reluctantly, and because of accommodation snags, rented a flat miles away, which meant we had to leave Rex in the kennels for a long time—this contributed to a miserable existence for him, as he loved his creature comforts.

Then, eventually, when all was said and done, we returned to the house for the first time since Dr Neilson's death. First, to gather any remaining possessions, if any, were still intact.

So thus, readers, there you have the full extent of my adventure-fuelled *story,* with the dramas, notations and paranormal intrigue.

Consequently, I think it wise to return to the **_PROLOGUE_**.

****

The old man Alfred represented the 1960s, for his passing ignited my quest to find proof about what transpires after death, though I did not realise it at the time.

1985, the year where I found myself now, would undoubtedly be a time I would never be able or allowed to forget for the rest of my days, no matter what other state of affairs emerged.

Dr Neilson's death and the horrifying images of *Mellissa* would haunt us forever.

I stood rooted to the spot in the lounge uneasily—sighed and recalled various *memories.*

The weather turned grey, and spots of rain tapped on the ground outside. Consequently, nature's goodbye caused puddles of water to swell on the charred carpet.

My wrist, broken during the paranormal encounter with

Mellissa, ached—even after nine months, a brutal reminder of the supernatural attack.

I heard Maria toot the car horn; she had no intention of accompanying us in the house and thus remained outside.

I studied the scene before composing myself. Then exited the living room and stood in the wrecked hallway. I took one last glance at what remained of the electronic equipment. And went to the doorway. After stepping into the open-air, I shut the boarded door and kicked it firmly. I hastened a few steps and examined the house's exterior, blackened with soot and charred brickwork from the fire. Also, all the windows were fixed shut with squared wood.

I released a heavy sigh and bowed with sorrow. Next, Maria wound down the passenger car window. 'Stephen. Ready to leave?'

'Yes. Love,' I replied in a melancholy tone.

I stirred with emotions and sauntered onward. I gazed at the ground and noticed glass, wires, and other debris lying everywhere—even after this length of time.

A small book lay ajar on the grass. I bent down and held it aloft—its pages waterlogged and torn due to the weather. But one page, opened by the wind and rain, stood out prominently in smudged ink. I moved it to my face and read a sentence on the page in a humble tone.

IF OUR BIRTH IS BUT A DREAM
THEN PERHAPS DEATH IS OUR REALITY

I, Stephen Reid, waited a minute before dropping the waterlogged item to the ground, and then I began my journey to the car.

The book rested on the wet grass, and a brisk wind rustled the remaining pages like an autumn leaf falling to the ground.

Suddenly, to the left, a smart-suited gentleman, who tipped his hat, greeted me. 'Sir! Oh, sir! Please forgive the impertinence. Y'know! Sorry. Caught ya! At such a sad moment.'

'No problem. Pray tell. Continue.'

'I represent a firm of solicitors. Producers. Who are thrilled by your adventure? They want advice. Expertise in Electronic Voice Phenomenon and Spiricom. For a movie. They say! Without your idea. The film industry—'

'—That's a kind offer!' I finished, pondering with reflection. 'And I'm indeed flattered. However, the answer is… Never! Never do I want to recall this escapade again. As of now! I'm officially retired! Goodbye, sir. And… may I add… Good luck with any project.' The man shrugged, sighed and shrank back, disappointed.

Then I entered the car. 'You, said "never", smiled Maria. 'Exactly… Honey.' I flashed a wink. 'No more Electronic Voice Phenomenon. Or Spiricom. And definitely, no movies!'

So, I glanced at the destroyed house—before Maria started the car, pressed the accelerator, and drove down the windswept road.

THE END

BIOGRAPHY

Nathan Toulane is an author, musician and filmmaker. He has contributed to various articles and magazines and has a long-standing interest in history, theology, and psychology.

VELVET BOOKS